CW00674787

SHE'S BURIED DEEP

AN ARTEMIS BLYTHE MYSTERY THRILLER

GEORGIA WAGNER

Text Copyright © 2022 Georgia Wagner

Publisher: Greenfield Press Ltd

The right of Georgia Wagner to be identified as author of the Work has been asserted in accordance with the Copyright, Designs and Patents Act 1988

All rights reserved.

The book is copyright material and must not be copied, reproduced, transferred, distributed, leased, licensed or publicly performed or used in any way except as specifically permitted in writing by the publishers, as allowed under the terms and conditions under which it was purchased or as strictly permitted by applicable copyright law. Any unauthorised distribution or use of this text may be a direct infringement of the author's and publisher's rights and those responsible may be liable in law accordingly.

'She's Buried Deep' is a work of fiction. Names, characters, businesses, organisations, places, events, and incidents either are the product of the author's imagination or are used fictitiously. Any resemblance to actual persons, living or dead, and events or locations is entirely coincidental.

CONTENTS

PROLOGUE:

And so she ran for her life.

Stumbling through the detritus, disturbing worn leaves and old boughs. Some freshly fallen branches crunched underfoot, while others—laden with mold and fungus—gave way like cardboard.

Her heart hammered, and Megan shot another look over her shoulder.

A dark shadow moved through the trees in hot pursuit. She cursed, lowered her head and put on an extra burst of speed, the terror in her chest making it difficult to breathe at this breakneck pace. Just over the ridge laden with pine needles and strewn with moss—she spotted the orange fabric of her tent.

Five days she'd wanted to camp in the misty Cascade Mountains. Five days she'd intended to prove to herself that she could live apart from the lap of luxury, avoiding the everyday creature comforts that burdened this generation.

No phone. No internet. No computers. No air-conditioning.

It had all seemed like such an exciting idea at the time.

And now she was running for her life.

Brambles snared at her clothing. Two layers of sweaters. Sweatpants. The nights had been colder than she'd anticipated. Her gloves—*shit.*

She'd left them back in the tent.

No food either...

That was what had attracted the damn bear, anyhow.

A grizzly? Black bear?

She didn't know. She'd only been warned to keep the most odoriferous of her meals downwind. The giant, eight-hundred pound monster behind her was charging gamely along, easily closing the distance. It had started fifty feet behind her. Now thirty.

A few more wild steps...

Twenty paces away.

She risked a glance over her shoulder. An elongated, light brown face with a thick, wet snuffling nose. Teeth the size of fingers and large eyes fixated on her. The creature looked *thinner* than she might have liked...

Fat bears were slow. Fat bears weren't famished.

This bear was fast and looked ravenous. In the brief glimpse she allowed herself, her hair clinging to her sweat-drenched face, she spotted the bear run *into* a tree. Not around. *Into.*

The tree cracked under the pressure, splinters exploded, and as the tree toppled, the bear just kept coming, still huffing and grunting and growling and disheveling the earth in its endless and rapid pursuit.

Megan had to make a choice.

Ten feet away. It was going to grab her. She knew she couldn't outrun a bear. She sprinted through the overgrown forest. Portions had recently been treated with controlled fires, melting away the underbrush and clearing a path so that she didn't stumble into overgrowth every two steps.

Along one side, off to her right, the mountain elevated sharply. Thick sheets of sheer stone served as a barricade against access.

To her left, after only a few paces, the slopes dipped sharply, creating a downward incline that was both precarious and lined with ash-singed trees. The scent of the ash, the residue of the controlled fires, now swirled around her, making her gag.

The ground cover was turning from lush green or mottled brown to desolate black and gray.

She no longer looked back; she could *hear* the bear panting heavily, snarling. Could practically *feel* droplets of slobber and warm, moist breath against her neck.

Couldn't go right. Too steep. Couldn't go left, too sharp of a fall. She'd snap every bone in her body.

Then again... the bear would do worse.

So, with a desperate shout, Megan flung herself to the side, taking two wild steps. She felt something slice past her, tearing through the first layer of her two sweaters.

But then she leapt to the side, plunging over the sharp drop, hitting the ground *hard,* her shoulder protesting in pain but immediately giving way to far more aches and scrapes and bruises and batterings. She tumbled, rolling rapidly down the mountain. She'd been aiming for a particularly *clear* section of the slope, where the recent controlled fires had cleared most obstacles.

But her stomach found sharp roots. Her wrist found a rock and *cracked.*

Her scream of pain was held back by the lack of air in her lungs from the constant bludgeoning as she spun downwards.

No time to even *see* where she was going. Everything was just a whirling blur of colors. And then—a brief glimpse. An absolutely *enormous*, burnt-out husk of a tree, facing towards her, like a linebacker on one of her father's teams.

She tried to scream. Not that it would have helped.

But her lips were now stained with dirt and leaves. She couldn't change direction. Couldn't do anything, wind whipping about, except to...

Crunch.

She slammed straight into the hollowed-out fir.

Darkness took her instantly. She groaned, shivering, eyes fluttering. The darkness came in and out. Her consciousness slowly returned like grains of sand slipping through an hourglass. Her breath came in irregular patterns, and for a moment, she simply lay on the forest floor, eyes closed, entirely motionless.

Thoughts of that horrible, furry monster and its muzzle lined with teeth were secondary now. She needed to get to her feet. She let out a faint huff of air, trying not to gasp in pain. Her left hand braced against the ground, but as she put pressure on it, she instantly screamed in pain.

She exhaled deeply, groaning through taut lips. She used her other hand, scrambling for a root—something to brace against.

She pushed up once more...

The item she'd grabbed hold of felt smooth. Not a root. She frowned, blinking blearily, blood pouring down the side of her face, her jaw aching, bruises now forming all along her body. She murmured a quiet prayer beneath her breath, just like her mother used to do all those years ago, kneeling by some white bench with thin cushioning, facing the front of that church. Megan didn't remember much of those prayers, and she knew she likely didn't do it properly. She missed her mother, missed—even—that small church. There had been a time the people in her small town had been a community. But things had changed with the Ghost-killer's reign of terror.

She shivered in memory, trying not to move too much, trying to focus on other things besides the horror of pain.

So instead, she closed her mouth, tasting a coppery taint.

She sat up now, blinking. Leaves fell from her body. Pine needles tumbled. She glanced at what she'd grabbed to hold herself up.

For a moment, she frowned, inhaling the scent of disheveled earth. The odor of the mud lingered on the air with the scent of ash. She winced, glancing up the slope again from which she'd tumbled.

Then, she glanced at her hand.

The round rock she'd grabbed to steady herself wasn't a rock at all.

It took her a second, staring at the black-charred thing. Gaping holes looked back at her. Ice dabbed at her spine. She froze, staring.

The skull stared back.

She yanked her hand back upon recognizing 5what she held and stumbled to her feet. The pain was still immense, her motions sloppy and slow. No further sign of the bear that had chased her, though. This was a pleasant relief. She had fallen too far, evidently, for the woodland monster to pursue her. But now, scrambling back, horror in her chest, she stared at the fire-darkened skull, and its leering glare.

There was something almost accusatory about those gaping eye sockets. Something that sent shivers down her spine. And so she continued to retreat, tripping backwards, and holding a shout. She stared at the ground and realized that some animal must have been through before her. The ground was torn, ripped up, and she realized roots were jutting out of the earth beneath the skull.

Except, the roots were pale, splintered in ways that she didn't believe trees could emulate. Despite herself, despite the terror, the pain, the exhaustion. The knowledge that she had no phone, lost somewhere in the Cascade Mountains, her curiosity prodded her forward. She knelt slowly, fingers trailing through the dirt.

Her heart hammered, pounding in her chest.

She poked at what she had taken for roots.

The dirt cleared beneath her insistently brushing fingertips. The ministrations of her curiosity, however, revealed a far more gruesome spectacle.

A rib cage. Weathered, rotten, and jutting up like some heinous shipwreck.

And there, trapped in the rib cage, half buried where some animal had attempted to get at them, were two more skulls. As if the rib cage itself was some horrible basket, and the skulls, like plucked fruit placed in its confines.

She held back a scream, this time turning, and refusing to look back.

The image was seared into her mind. Gnaw marks on the rib bones. Some creature had tried to reach those skulls. One skull on the earth, previously exhumed. Two, somehow, trapped in that rib cage, where it had been used to protect them from the elements.

Three dead. Three corpses.

No phone, and so all Megan could do was run. For even the briefest moment, she forgot about the bear lurking in the woods. Forgot about the pain lancing down her broken wrist. Forgot about the bruises covering her beaten and bludgeoned form.

She just ran. She was far too scared to scream.

CHAPTER 1

Artemis remained standing, facing the bullet-proof glass, shifting back and forth, and trying not to look *too* nervous. Her foot tapped a tattoo against the prison's cold, concrete floor. Her breath faintly dabbed at the glass, misting it, so she took a step back, refusing to give the man the satisfaction that perhaps his presence had increased her breathing patterns.

She was here on a mission.

She'd found out what her father had been doing with Baker—the reason behind those postcards.

Knowing this... knowing that she had snipped this strand of web woven by her old man, she allowed herself a small, grim smile. *Celebrate the small victories. It's momentum.* Often, she would recollect small sayings her sister Helen had uttered when the two of them had been under the same roof.

Helen had disappeared some seventeen years ago. There were those that rumored she was her father's first victim, her body buried somewhere in the Misty Cascade Mountains behind the small town of Pinelake.

But Artemis refused to believe this. Her sister had been her best friend. Hell, her *only* friend for many years, until she moved in with the Kramers. Jamie Kramer had been part of the reason she'd accepted the FBI's consulting offer officially.

You should take it.

She'd never thought four small words could be so maddening. But Jamie had wanted her back in Pinelake, had wanted her back in Seattle.

She shook her head, trying not to think of the cryptic text messages they'd been exchanging over the last few days. It felt like some odd dance in which she didn't know the moves.

Now that she'd come back to Seattle, accepting Agent Grant's offer, things had *changed* somewhat.

But one thing hadn't...

Her loathing of the Ghost-killer and everything he'd poisoned.

Because that was the answer, wasn't it? She glanced down at the briefcase she'd rested on the floor. Working with the FBI had come with perks. Agent Wade had organized this new meeting with her old man. It was enough to almost make her forget about the upcoming blitz tournament, where the current world champion, Anton Radesh, would be participating. She'd spent much of her adult life preparing for an opportunity like this. Opportunities in chess tournaments were few and far between.

She shifted uncomfortably, shooting a glance towards one of the prison guards behind the glass—he was eyeing her, his gaze lingering just a second too long before bouncing away. It was the small details she most paid attention to.

People lied with their lips. It was much, much harder to lie with one's eyes.

In fact, it was often Artemis' eyes that most attracted the attention of men. One of her eyes, like moonlit frost, the other hazel-gold. Mismatched from birth. She also had striking features. Some loathed her for being pretty. But she tried to accommodate such opinions as best she could. As a tournament chess player, running a circuit dominated by men, she'd done her best not to antagonize with her appearance; no makeup, simple ponytail, soap instead of perfume. *One enemy at a time.*

Another one of Helen's admonishments.

Artemis brushed her coal-black hair behind an ear. Her pale skin never fared well in the sunlight—perhaps that was why she found herself so often coming back to the misty, overcast northwest.

The guard pretended like he wasn't watching now. Thankfully, he was distracted by his job. The man turned quickly, reaching for a metal handle to a very thick, brown-painted steel door. The door buzzed behind the bulletproof glass, and as a familiar figure emerged, she straightened somewhat, eyes narrowed, watching as her father approached.

His dark blue prison uniform displayed his name and prisoner number in stitched, black letters across his lapels. His neat hair was brushed to the side, notably longer than one might have expected in a maximum security prison, but Artemis knew her father always found some way to bend the rules.

He'd made his living as a mentalist, after all—posing as a true psychic for years.

The silver-haired man carried himself like a lawyer or some hedge fund manager. There was something intentionally *distinguished* about his posture, about his gait, about the pleasant way in which he greeted guards who stared at him in stony silence.

Her father had always known how to put on a show. He'd been the one to teach his offspring how to pay attention to postures—how to spot even the smallest details.

Most people lied with their lips, but not with their bodies.

Her father was a master liar with both. Every twitch, every step, every smile, even the twinkling in his eyes, an intentional outfit, like some sort of mask constructed for that very moment.

In fact, Artemis wasn't sure she'd ever *met* the real Otto. The charade with her old man never ended.

As he approached the glass, he did so with an energetic, lively stride. He nodded to one of the guards, winking. "Thank you, Max," he said.

The guard glared back.

Her father's voice was as she remembered it so often. Humorous, good-natured, charming. Always charming. A voice verged on sudden belly-laughs and controlled chuckles. A voice that whispered *tell me a joke, and I'll reward your efforts.*

Even in the tone, the voice *asked* to be catered to, demanded some type of performance.

And so Artemis couldn't hold her temper. Her father acted like he was some doting business magnate, deigning to condescend to greet his favored employees. She refused to let him get away with it.

"I know what you did," she said simply, speaking loud enough to redirect her old man's attention. She had intended to jar him.

But it was credit to her father's abilities that he didn't so much as glance at her until he was good and ready.

He hesitated a moment, cleared his throat, and then slowly turned, watching her with an amused smile.

"Hello, Artemis," he said. "What a pleasant surprise. Come, sit." He gestured towards the chair in the visitor's area, on the opposite side of his own. Otto was lowered—somewhat forcefully—into his own chair, but he didn't resist, and instead leaned back, crossing his legs as if he were simply visiting the barber.

Artemis remained standing, staring at him. "I already spoke with the warden," she said simply. "They ran tests at the lab, on my request."

He looked at her, puzzled. "What on earth are you talking about?"

She kept her expression impassive, refusing to rise to the bait of the condescending tone. He was always pivoting, always looking for a way in.

She said, quietly, "The postcards were laced with hallucinogenics. There were no notes, nothing in the letters themselves. It was the paper you wanted. An old trick. You had Joseph Baker soak the postcards, dry them, and send them to you. Then you used the drug-soaked paper as currency in here. Bribing people. Maybe even some guards. That's how you've been getting information. That's how you've been coercing people to tell you what they know."

She spoke quickly, dispassionately, like some medical professional delivering bad news about a terminal illness. But she would have been lying if she had said there wasn't pleasure in the accusation. Even as she spoke, though, her father maintained his mask. He didn't blink, didn't gasp. He didn't react at all. After she had finished, he gave a small, confused smile.

"My friend, Joseph Baker? I hear that you were involved in arresting him again. He's a good man, Artemis, you should have some compassion."

She pointed at him, her finger jamming towards the glass. She held back a sudden retort, though. It was rich for this man to lecture her about compassion.

She didn't want to spend another second with him. She wanted him to know, though. That was how he had been bribing, coercing, and gathering information. A steady stream of currency, more valuable than money or gold in a place like this. Drugs. A temporary, pleasurable reprieve from the horrors of maximum security, surrounded by men like...

Her father.

"I don't need you to admit it," she said simply. "The tests were already done." She reached into her briefcase, tugged at the latch, unhooked it, and then pulled out a fist full of postcards. She waved them at her father, raising her eyebrows. "We did a count on how many postcards were sent, against how many were confiscated. You used about half of them. These, though?" She waved them as if fanning her face, "I bet it really hurt when they took them from your cell. Also, I know about Easy."

"Hmm?" An innocent little tilt of his head.

"We've already had the warden questioning others who you bribed. Easy—the name of a guard you're working with, right?" Artemis gave a smug little nod. The two guards behind her father shifted uncomfortably. Artemis concluded with, "One way or another, we're going to find out who's in your pocket. And *what* you've been feeding him. It's only a matter of time." She allowed herself a small, triumphant smile.

Her father studied her now, and said, in a hurt voice, "I don't know about *any* of that. You look angry, Artemis. It's not good for your blood pressure. Why are you mad at me? Do you want me to suffer?" There was a pleading quality to his voice and a sadness to his eyes.

It troubled her, deeply, how easily her father could turn it on.

She scowled at the man. She especially scowled when she realized a couple of the guards, watching the situation, were starting to glance at her with judgmental looks. As if wondering, why she was taunting the helpless old man.

The guards, likely, didn't even know they were reacting to her father's emotions. Didn't realize they were being played, and that the stage he had set up was serving its purpose.

But the way they leaned, the change in their postures, the amount of time they spent watching their prisoner, against watching her. When they had first entered, they had watched her out of some sense of attraction, or interest. But now, they kept glancing between the two. Even prison guards could manage sympathy. Not much, not really. But in moments of control, with no threat around them, when they simply had to watch and listen, they were trained, by television, by books, by movies, to form opinions.

And it was this very sense that her father played on.

She was now being cast as the heartless FBI agent, the daughter who loathed her own father.

He was casting himself as the charming, misunderstood man, who had rehabilitated himself in prison.

It was all an act, all pretend.

"They're destroying the other postcards," she said simply. "So if you owe anyone, let them know, Otto, the payments have dried up. Hopefully, it doesn't get you hurt."

As she said it, she realized she was playing into the roles cast for her. She also realized she didn't much care.

She wasn't here to make friends. She was here for another reason, though. Now that she had found out how her father had been funneling influence into the prison in the form of currency, it answered questions about things he had known. Not completely, but Artemis knew that prisoners weren't the only ones susceptible to greed. If even one guard had bene-fited from Otto's scheme with Joseph Baker, then that would have been a source of information outside the prison.

She had told the warden this as well. He had been far less amenable to this suggestion.

She sighed. The second reason she had come by, though, was a promise she had made to herself. The last case, in Chicago, had proven to her that not everything was as it seemed. She knew that already. With a family like hers, she had always known that.

But now, she felt especially certain.

And she'd promised herself that she would look into Helen's disappearance. There was a chance her sister was still alive. Her father had suggested as much, hadn't he?

She studied him, tilting her head slowly, considering how best to word her next question without cluing him into what she really wanted.

Otto stared back, watching her just as closely. And then...

He smiled a crocodile grin. A smile she'd seen before, es-pecially when center-stage, staring out at an audience. It was the same sort of smile Artemis often saw across the table, in a tournament. It only ever appeared on her chess opponents' faces when they had *won* and knew it.

She braced as Otto said, "You're here to ask me about Helen."

It wasn't a question.

She didn't blink. She'd been prepared for this... though... not how *quickly* he'd reached the conclusion. She hadn't even mentioned her sister.

Otto was nodding though, smiling. "Yes, yes—you're here for her. Well, Artemis—does that mean you know I'm innocent? I didn't kill anyone." His voice shifted again, and now his eyes brimmed with tears. He stared through the glass, his voice trembling. "P-please, daughter. My dear, dear daughter. I love you. You know I do. Listen to me! This place is hell. I—I can't sleep. I barely eat. Men here want to hurt me, Artemis! No—no don't scowl at me. Please, I'm an innocent man!" His voice choked. His lips cracked a sob. "I've been arrested for crimes I never committed! I *never* killed Helen! Someone else did! Someone took her—kidnapped her! Find Helen. Find her Artemis and clear my name!"

His tears, his shaking voice, might have been more convincing if Artemis hadn't seen the evidence herself. One particularly damning piece had been the corpse of a woman he'd killed in bed with him.

She scowled at her old man.

"If Helen is alive, if you really didn't hurt her... then where is she?"

Her father straightened, swallowing. "I know you think I'm a monster, my dear child. But even if so..." he looked at her, his eyes piercing. "I'm not the only monster in those mountains. This place... this dark place... It's sick, Artemis. Very sick.

16

People do just..." he shook his head, wrinkling his nose. "The *worst* things. You won't *believe* the sorts that are in this prison with me, Artemis. You have to find Helen. Find who took her. Clear my name, dear! Please! I'm begging you! Have a heart!"

She could feel her temper still rising. Could feel disgust at every uttered word from her old man's mouth. She hated just how brazenly he played with emotions as if they were toys in a pram. Hated the way that she never knew what was true and what wasn't.

She didn't trust him. Not one bit.

In fact, listening to him, she now felt *less* confident that Helen might be alive.

Her father had killed Helen, hadn't he? All the other victims, all the rest had been very similar to Helen. Beauties, geniuses, academically gifted... The targets had been like his daughter.

But that had always been the question.

Had he killed Helen, then gone on a rampage reenacting the murders?

Or had someone else hurt Helen, taken her... and then had her father broken over it, enacting his grief on his helpless victims?

There were other options too, and Artemis refused to leave any stone unturned. She shivered, standing there, staring at the man with tears in his eyes. Perhaps the part she hated most was how, completely unbidden, her own emotions tried to bubble to the surface.

She *felt* compassion. A dirty compassion. One that she hadn't wanted but that he'd conjured, reaching into her soul, plucking it and pulling out to display in a sort of humiliating exposure. Counterfeit, stolen emotions.

She scowled all the more, began to turn. This had hardly been a fruitful visit. But at least her father knew.

As she buttoned her briefcase, though...

Her phone began to vibrate in her pocket. She frowned, turning away from the glass now, facing the exit. It felt good to put her back to her father.

"Artemis!" he was saying. "Please, have a heart! Don't make your old daddy beg!"

She heard other voices through the speaker behind her. "Come, Mr. Blythe. Time to leave!"

She began walking away, refusing to look back. Her phone met her ear, and somehow, it felt like a lifeline. She felt a surge of relief to have someone, *anyone*, else to talk to.

Part of her, a small part—or perhaps larger than she would admit—had hoped Jamie Kramer would be on the line.

But instead, it was another familiar voice.

"Hey, Checkers."

"Forester?"

"Mhmm—first shot. Look, you're in the area yeah?"

"Ummm. Yes. I've been at the apartment Grant rented for me. But I didn't think training started until next week."

"No, don't worry about that," Forester said. Agent Cameron Forester was one of the FBI agents she'd worked with in the past. Another dangerous man. But at least... for the moment, he was dangerous on the same side. Now, though, his words were strange. Almost... almost emotional.

She frowned at the tone.

"Shit, Checkers, we're going all hands on deck for this one. We got a case in your backyard. About fifty miles down the mountain range."

"A case?" she perked up, keeping her voice low and waiting for the door to buzz as another guard allowed her back out of the visitor's area.

"Yeah... a big one. Bodies found on the slopes. Bunch of them. Looks like a mass grave. Anyway, I'll send you coordinates. You got that rental car, still?"

"Yeah... Yeah, I'm on my way. Wait, Cameron," Artemis said, moving through the hall, towards the prison's main atrium. "Where in the mountains?"

"Hmm... near Leavenworth. IN their backyard."

Artemis felt a cold chill at these words.

Her father had been notorious for leaving his victims on the mountain slopes. Sometimes buried, sometimes left for animals to pick clean. Once he was done with them, he disposed of them like rubbish.

More bodies, though?

Her father's work?

Or someone else...

I'm not the only monster in those mountains...

Her father's words echoed in her mind and left her with a greasy sensation along her skin. Other monsters? Or the same?

And whose remains had been found?

Artemis felt another horrible thought rise to the surface... What if her search for Helen had ended as quickly as it had started?

Missing seventeen years... the likelihood of her still being alive was very low. Artemis knew it.

Chances were, Helen Blythe was buried in those mountains.

What if they'd just found the grave?

"I'm coming," Artemis said quickly. "D-do... Do we have IDs for the victims?"

"Not yet. Working on it. Come quick—shit. Grant's yelling at me. Coming!" Forester's voice called out, quieter now, suggesting he'd lowered the phone.

Artemis picked up her pace and was practically jogging by the time she reached the atrium and moved through the security detail towards the sliding glass doors out into the parking lot

CHAPTER 2

The scent of ash lingered on the mountain top, and Artemis waved a hand in front of her face to clear the breeze. The drive from the prison had *not* been a pleasant one.

Airports weren't the only thing Artemis hated; driving, in its own right, was an entirely unpleasant experience. Not because she didn't trust herself behind the wheel. But because she didn't trust anyone else.

Now, though, the bad taste left by the journey to the mountain was replaced by a slow dread.

Already, at least twenty figures in FBI jackets were moving around the scene. Local police were there; Artemis was relieved to see that she didn't recognize any of the officers. This part of the Cascades was beyond the jurisdiction of the Pinelake police department.

Agent Forester stood next to his partner, Agent Desmond Wade. The two men had stony expressions as they stared into the ever-widening pit. Mounds of earth were being carted away in wheelbarrows. A portion of the forest floor had been cleared, allowing for black tarps draped across the ground.

Bones were placed upon these tarps as they were found.

Currently, seven skulls leered at the sky.

Artemis tried not to stare at the fragments of skeletons. Tried not to think about Helen. She stood a few paces behind Agent Forester, watching, frowning.

Agent Forester shot a quick glance back at her, shaking his head which only further disheveled his untended hair, as if he'd never so much as heard of a comb. He was a tall man—nearly six foot four, with handsome features, dark eyes and a left ear lumpy from a professional fighting career.

His eyes were perpetually amused as if thinking of some secret joke, but now those same eyes were scowling at the bones.

"Seven so far," he said slowly. "One over there without a head yet."

Artemis came to a stop next to him, staring. "Eight victims?"

"So far," Forester murmured. "Forensics is still on its way. Traffic jam." He snorted, suggesting he didn't think very much of anyone who got caught in traffic.

Cameron Forester wore mismatched socks, one of them brown with red dots, the other one bright pink. His suit was an attempt to blend in as a true professional, but not a very *good* attempt. For one, he had a tattoo just visible past his collar, climbing under his neck. For another, he *never* seemed capable of properly buttoning the suit. The bottom two buttons were misaligned, and Artemis was beginning to think Forester did this on purpose.

The thick scar along Forester's palm was pale, and crawled up his wrist and forearm before disappearing under an unbuttoned sleeve. Forester often reminded Artemis of some sort of free-spirit attempting to camouflage himself in appropriate attire.

Now, though, his usual humor, his usual cavalier attitude was muted. He was shaking his head and murmuring to Wade. Desmond had raised his camera, aiming it towards the pit, taking quick photos of the bones.

"Where's Agent Grant?" Artemis said, swallowing a lump.

"Hmm—oh, umm, Auntie is on her way," Forester said. "Apparently eight bodies is enough to cancel a trip to the salon."

"Wait, really?"

He snorted. "Nah. Any thoughts, Checkers?"

"On—on this?"

"Mhmm."

"I... I don't really know." Artemis paused, going quiet, allowing herself to think before responding. Neither of them spoke for a good sixty seconds. She studied the bones, studied the angle of the mountain, the scorched earth.

"A fire," she said simply.

"Controlled fire," Forester replied. "Intentional. Cleared out some of the brush which was stacking up like kindling."

Artemis frowned, glancing up the mountain slope. It had taken her thirty minutes just to *reach* this spot off the road. Her car was currently parked along the shoulder, along with a fleet of FBI vehicles.

"Whoever did this," she said quietly, "went to a lot of trouble to hide the bodies."

"Yeah," Forester said slowly. "Used that big ol' tree as a sign post."

Artemis frowned, staring at the tree under which the bones had been discovered. "Who found them?"

"Some camper. Says she got chased by a bear, literally fell into it."

"Huh. Is she okay?"

"Bruised up. Limp wrist. Should be fine—they took her to the hospital."

Artemis nodded, still scanning the area, frowning as she did. The two largest trees in the area were both within twenty feet of each other. With branches reaching towards the sky far above, the trunk so wide it would have been able to swallow a sedan whole.

The tree was rotten, scorched and hollowed out, though. No leaves in the branches, just dead wood.

She glanced off to the second *larger* tree, about twenty paces in front of the mass burial site. "What about that one?" she murmured.

"Hmm? That tree? What about it."

"Why choose this smaller one."

"I don't know."

Artemis paused once more, again allowing silence to linger between them. Then, after a few seconds, she said, "Why bury the bodies here. He chose the tree because he would be able to find it, right?"

"Right, so what's your point?"

Artemis didn't speak now, but instead began studying the tree next to them. She didn't glance at the roots, nor did she look at the hollowed section at the base, but instead, her eyes moved up towards the taller section of the tree. It had always impressed her how such an enormous thing could grow slowly, over the course of decades, sometimes centuries.

There were many bodies. At least eight. In her experience, from what she had learned studying the minds of killers, it was evident that bodies took time to pile up. Even her father had taken a couple of years to kill his victims.

"How old are the bodies?" Artemis said slowly.

Agent Wade glanced at her, hesitant. The ex-Special Forces operative had a sharp jaw, sharp cheekbones, and even a brow line that looked as if it had been carved from granite. He wasn't quite handsome, but he certainly wasn't ugly. He looked like an angry action hero, broad-shouldered and muscled, suggesting he spent a decent amount of time at the gym. Also, he was wearing sunglasses, which he always seemed to wear, both inside and out.

The man often reminded Artemis of a pit bull. She had heard, in confidence, that Agent Wade was Forester's fifth partner—four others having quit. Wade was patient, despite his appearance, and didn't seem all that bothered by Cameron's usual antics. The two of them, apparently, had made a good team over the years they had worked together.

Now, Wade, who rarely spoke, said, "Still waiting. Photos I sent to the coroner got an initial dating of twenty years."

He wiggled his phone and continued to watch her, as if curious what sort of reaction this would earn.

Artemis blinked. "Twenty years? These bodies were buried twenty years ago?"

"Some of them," said Wade. "But that's just a guess based on a high-definition photo. Forensics should be here soon."

Cameron scowled. "How much longer?"

"Ten minutes."

"That's what they're saying? Yeah right. They said that half an hour ago."

Wade did not reply.

25

Artemis continued to scan the tree now, her eyes moving higher. "Were all the bodies buried twenty years ago?"

"Probably not," Wade said. "A couple of them still have meat on their bones."

Artemis felt like she was going to be sick. She inhaled shakily, counting to herself, and then exhaled.

She could faintly feel a knot forming in her stomach. Anxiety could come in all forms. But in her case, it came in the form of panic attacks. Debilitating excursions into unpleasant emotions50 that often entailed living out memories long forgotten.

And so she took a moment, steadying her breathing, inhaling, exhaling.

"What is it?" Forester asked.

"What?" She said, absentmindedly.

"You've got that look in your eyes. Care to share with the class?"

"I'm just," she trailed off, frowning, "thinking."

"That's a good thing."

"Maybe you should teach Cam sometime," Wade said.

Cameron nodded, chuckling, "Look who has jokes."

But Artemis ignored them both, ignored the phone in agent Wade's hand. Ignored the look of amusement on Forester's face. Twenty years. How tall could a tree grow in twenty years?

She began to move, glancing back up the slope. But then, with a frown, she turned the other way, beginning to descend the steep incline, careful, occasionally reaching out with her hand to steady herself. She moved around the opposite side of the tree. Still staring towards the higher branches.

And that's when she spotted it. The fire hadn't reached that high. There, about fifteen feet above where she had originally been looking, she spotted a deep gash.

As if someone had taken to it with an axe. Chunks of the tree were missing, but the cuts were not fresh. The breeze had blown some of the ash into these cuts, but otherwise, sap, age, and growth had slowly tried to cover them.

But they were still visible.

Artemis paused for a moment, and then called out, "Up there, see that?"

Agent Wade remained where he was, waving his phone and muttering, "If I move, I lose my signal."

But Forester approached, frowning at her, and watching.

As he drew near, his eyes moved up the tree as well, settling on the indicated branch. "What exactly am I looking at?"

She didn't have to answer, though. A few seconds after he had asked, his eyes landed on the indicated markings. He paused, gave a faint whistle, and said, "Huh. Nice eye." He then shot her a quick look. "How did you know it was there?" And again, before she could answer, he replied to his own question. "Of course... because you're—"

"I'm *not* psychic. No, look... he would have needed a quick way to remember where he'd buried the others, yes? Unless we think he just buried them all at once. But that's not the case if some are newer than others."

"Huh. So you think he marked the tree to find it."

"Second largest tree in the area. Marked it to find it... Yeah, I think he left himself a sign post."

Forester paused. "Second largest?"

"Mhmm. That one over there is bigger."

"Why... why choose the *second* largest. Seems weird, somehow."

Artemis nodded quietly, her eyes had moved to the largest tree, twenty paces away. She stared at it, eyes moving up the branches as well. Then, she went very still.

"What?"

"I... I think I know why he chose the second largest tree."

"Why's that?"

Artemis let out a faint sigh. "Because maybe he ran out of room."

"What?"

She pointed, and again Forester followed her gaze. She was indicating another, identical mark in the tallest tree. This time, though, the mark was even higher up. An older mark then... *years older.* Which meant...

She felt a faint shiver along her arms, and her hand moved, pointing towards the base of this largest tree. "Y-you need to dig there," she said, her voice sounding hollow. The knot of anxiety had returned to her chest.

Forester was frowning. "What, at that other tree?"

"Yes... Yes, I think you should dig there too."

Forester paused, then shrugged. "Fine by me... Say, Checkers, what did you mean he *ran out of room?*"

Artemis tried to reply, but she'd lost her voice briefly. The air was caught in her throat, her lungs depleting. She just stared at this tree, glanced at the eight corpses on the black tarps, then moved her gaze towards this second marked fir.

"I hope I'm wrong," she murmured.

But the dread in her chest suggested otherwise.

CHAPTER 3

Forensics had arrived in time for the discovery of the second mass burial site. Agent Wade had grabbed a shovel right
alongside some of the forensic grunts and was dumping earth
off the side of the slope, helping to reveal more bones.

Nine more bodies had been discovered.

"Seventeen," Forester murmured at Artemis' side. He shook
his head. "Been some time since I had a case with this many
dead." He gave a low whistle, massaging the back of his knuckles. "Think the same guy did them in?"

Artemis stood by him, watching as the ranks of the FBI and
local law enforcement swelled. More figures in blue jackets
or white gear were moving down the slope in careful fashion,
approaching the two trees.

Suddenly, Agent Wade looked up. "Hey," he said, somehow
managing to add a grunt on the end of the exclamation.

"What is it?" Forester shot back. Leaves crunched as the tall
agent adjusted his posture, then stepped over a tangle of large
roots to stand nearer the hole where Wade worked.

In answer, Wade slammed his shovel into the ground.

"Umm... nice form?" Forester guessed.

"No, shut up asshole—not that. *This.*" Another slice into the dirt, which ended in a loud *thunk.*

Forester hesitated. "You found a root?"

"Not roots."

"Huh—what is that?" Forester leaned in, peering over the disheveled earth.

Artemis approached as well, peering past the man into the earth. A few more bones had already been removed from this particular section, but Wade had gone even deeper.

And there, laying through the earth, she spotted a wooden beam of rotten wood.

"What is that?" Forester said, dropping to his haunches.

Artemis stared, though, feeling a flicker of anxiety. "That's a support beam from a mineshaft," she said. "There used to be all sorts in these parts. Old run-down mines covered up by the government."

"A mineshaft? What sort of mine?"

Artemis wrinkled her nose, thinking back as far as she could. "Hmm... Gold, silver, I think. Eighteen hundreds maybe? Jamie Kramer would know more—he's a bit of a buff for local history."

"Jamie who?" said Forester.

"The guy from that other case," Wade shot back. He cleared his throat, lowering his voice and glancing awkwardly at Artemis. "Umm, you shot his... you know."

"Oh, his dad?"

Wade grimaced.

Artemis didn't meet his gaze. She'd been there when Mr. Kramer had been killed. She'd never had the chance to properly apologize to Jamie for her involvement. He'd been the one to reinitiate contact. In a way, the two of them were more similar now than before.

Both of them with killer fathers. Jamie had lost his mother and father in one fell swoop. Now he took care of his baby sister.

She felt for the man. But even if she'd been able to go back in time, she wasn't sure how she could have done anything differently.

Sometimes, even the best moves led to checkmate.

Thunk. Agent Wade swung the shovel again, shaking his head. "Gotta find the entrance to this thing. No coincidence."

"You don't think so?" Forester queried.

"Nah. Buncha bones on top of an old mineshaft? Gotta be related."

"Sure... I mean, maybe. Still don't even know how these folks were wasted."

"Yes we do!" said a voice behind them, calling out sweetly.

All of them turned, facing a woman who was approaching them with something of a skip in her step. She had a single, white earbud in one ear and was humming along with the music—it sounded like some sort of upbeat gospel track.

Artemis instantly felt more cheerful as Dr. Miracle Bryant drew near. The coroner was quite round but moved with grace and agility—granted, the last time Artemis had encountered the woman, she'd been prancing and pirouetting around two corpses in her sparkled and artistically adorned coroner's lab. Now, as she drew near, the sparkles were reserved for two dangling earrings which flashed and glittered as she approached. Her hair was no longer dark, streaked with pink, but instead had turned a bright green color and was pulled back behind her ears in a no-nonsense ponytail.

The rest of Dr. Bryant was very much in favor of nonsense.

She had a pink, sparkling flower stenciled on the lapel of her white coat. Her fingernails were each painted a different marvelous hue, with miniature paintings of flowers and the like in the center of the paint. Her wide hips did a sort of shimmy along with the music as she approached, but she nearly tripped as she moved on the steep terrain and she adopted a more cautious, and far safer, stride which involved a shuffle, a pause, a few kicks to clear sticks, then another shuffling step.

Like this, and waving a clipboard in one hand, she reached the three figures. "Hello!" she said excitedly. "Ms. Blythe, Agent Forester and... I don't believe we've had the pleasure, but my—aren't you handsome!" She extended a gloved hand towards Wade.

Wade glanced down at the glove, then up again. "Have you been touching dead things with that?"

"What—oh, dear Lord—so, so sorry." She flashed a magnetic smile, which started in her eyes and escaped through her curled lips and flashing white teeth. She lowered her hand but then waved it towards the bodies on the plastic. "Our poor dears were all killed the same way," she said. "I didn't mean to eavesdrop of course, Agent Forester."

Artemis was impressed the coroner had remembered their names—they'd only met once, after all. Behind the buttoned up white coat, Artemis glimpsed a t-shirt that displayed stampeding ponies with brightly colored hair flying over rainbows.

She hid a smile and focused on the somber words being spoken.

"Some sort of sharp object... Multiple puncture wounds on most of the victims. Some it's hard to tell, and I won't know until we have our darlings back home, but the weapon has similar markings. Ah—see, look here."

She stooped now, huffing as if the exertion of bending over was costly, but then steadied herself and pointed towards a large femur resting on a black mat. "This one is a defensive wound, I believe. But see?"

Artemis leaned in, and also spotted the indicated gouge mark.

"Huh," Forester said. "Not a knife."

"No, no, sweetie," said the middle-aged coroner. "Not a knife."

"Stiletto?"

"That, I'm afraid, I can't say. But... hmm... the wound sort of curves, see that—wait, actually, sorry this is my favorite part." Dr. Bryant held up a finger and pressed her earbud in, closing her eyes, smiling brightly and humming along to a tune. After a few seconds where the rest of them all stood awkwardly, she opened her eyes again.

Artemis remembered why she'd liked the vibrant coroner the last time they'd met.

Dr. Bryant nodded, glancing at them again. "Sorry, what was I saying."

Forester pointed at the nearest corpse. "Wounds... not a knife."

"Yes... well, I'll have a better idea when I can get home and take some photos. We have quite a few guests coming over, as I'm sure you can see." She sighed softly, murmuring something beneath her breath and shaking her head. "What a waste... But

I also should mention the victims are women. Oldest I can tell at first glance is sixty."

"Were any of them late teens?" Artemis said quickly. Again, the image of Helen flashed through her mind, accompanied by those bronze curls and kind eyes.

"I'll get back to you on that, dear. I... I don't see any prepubescents. Thank God for that."

"Not sure I want to thank anyone," Forester muttered, staring at the mound of bones.

"Ah... yes... well... you may have a point. Hmm—alright. Wonderful! I'll let you know what else I find, Ms. Blythe, Mr. Forester. And... I again don't believe I have your name."

"Agent Wade."

"Ah, yes—a beautiful name to match that beautiful jawline, hmm?" She gave a little purring sound in her throat, winked a long paste-on eyelash, and then bustled off, shuffle-shoving more leaves out of her path as she approached another row of corpses.

Wade blinked after her.

Forester muttered, "Want her number?"

"Shut up, Cam."

"Just saying. I think she's your type."

Wade just shook his head, glancing at Artemis. Forester also turned away from teasing his partner, watching Artemis as well.

She hesitated, swallowed, and blinked back and forth between them. "What?"

"Well?" Forester said.

Wade just frowned.

"Well, what?" Artemis asked.

Wade glanced at Forester then back at her, he left his shovel and wiped a hand across his dark, sweaty forehead.

Forester scratched at his chin. He then leaned in, "Are you getting any premonitions? Any... *sense?*"

"God dammit, Forester—I'm *not* psychic! No!" She huffed, glanced off, down the slopes again. She considered what Dr. Bryant had said. Most of the victims were women. No confirmation if any of them were in their late teens.

What if one of them was Helen after all?

Artemis scowled, closing her eyes, *thinking.*

Sometimes, movement *felt* like progress but only served as a distraction. She hesitated again, glanced up the slope, at the trees, then murmured, "The killer never came from that road."

"What?" Forester said.

She pointed towards the road where most of the security vehicles were parked. Where the woman who'd found the bones had stumbled down. "The killer didn't come from that way when burying them."

"How do you know that?"

"Because... look at the marks on the trees again. You can only see them if you're coming from the south, *not* the north."

"So you think he trekked up here? Up the slope?6"

"Yes. That's exactly what I think."

Forester glanced at Wade, back at Artemis, then Wade again. "Wanna keep diggin' big guy, or go for a hike?"

Wade shook his head, returning his attention to his shovel. Another *swish thunk* as he hit the wooden beam. He cursed, repositioning to avoid the rotten wood.

"I've got another one!" someone suddenly shouted.

Eyes turned, blue jackets quivered like water in a storm. A young lab tech was waving a skull over his head from the other side of the tree Wade was digging at. The lab tech sheepishly lowered his arm as Dr. Bryant yelped and hurried over, fluttering her hand to get him to stop brandishing the thing.

Wade continued digging.

Forester glanced at Artemis. "Hike?"

She sighed but nodded. "Sure... The killer came from that way. It's the best line of sight of the trees and their markings."

"Got it, boss. Lead the way."

Artemis hesitated, glancing across the gruesome scene of ashen forest floor, unearthed corpses and hollow trees. She shook her head, muttered slowly and then began to move, careful not to fall, taking the slope in cautious, incremental footsteps, and deeply dreading what she might find at the bottom.

CHAPTER 4

It was Forester who nearly fell into the open mineshaft, and Artemis was glad for the reprieve. She leaned against a boulder, breathing heavily and feeling the warmth pulse along her arms and chest.

Forester, meanwhile, cursed, tugging at an old, toppled log, trying to dislodge himself from where his foot had punctured the ground cover.

"What in the hell," he snapped.

Artemis hurried over across the leafy floor, reaching out and snagging Forester's arm. Where her fingers snatched at his disheveled suit, she felt a buzz up her hand. As Forester managed to yank his leg from the sudden hole, she took a quick step back, lowering her hand

It was only then that she realized she found herself lost in the deep wilderness with a self-proclaimed sociopath.

Anti-social personality disorder. That's what Forester and Wade had said. The ex cage-fighter was an odd amalgam of cavalier while living by-the-seat-of-his-pants, and also unspeakably deadly. Artemis had once seen Forester beat up a room full of thugs in a jeweler's shop.

He called himself "ataraxic," suggesting the portion of his brain that was meant to process fear didn't work properly. Unable to help herself, Artemis had looked up the condition online and had found out that it was a sign of anti-social personality disorder to sense little to no emotional fear when confronted by certain situations that might otherwise terrify a person. In addition, while sociopaths generally couldn't form emotional connections with people, sometimes there were instances where they *could* form very strong emotional ties to one or two specific people.

Perhaps someone in their past who had meant something to them, who they had enmeshed with, or, perhaps, someone who reminded them of that person.

It was a strange thing now to realize suddenly how vulnerable she felt, standing in the woods with a man who possessed a similar psychological makeup as some of the people they hunted.

Artemis shivered a bit, lingering back and frowning at Forester. He'd been protective in the past—often helpful. But she couldn't forget to keep attentive.

It didn't help that he was tall and handsome and had that wry smile that made his eyes crinkle in the corners.

"You good, Checkers?"

"I'm fine—you? Did you hurt your ankle?"

Forester shrugged sheepishly, shaking his foot, and hopping in place, disheveling leaves and further revealing the opening in the forest floor.

Artemis stepped forward again, distracted by her own curiosity. There, in the mud and beneath old, dead detritus, she spotted a lichen-garbed post. A similar, moldered beam to the one Agent Wade had discovered beneath the mass grave.

"Forester," Artemis said slowly, "Look." She extended her foot somewhat timidly, clearing the refuse and revealing the edge of the opening.

Forester whistled. "Well, I'll be... Think that leads to Wonderland?"

"I think maybe we've found the opening to our killer's gold mine."

"Huh. The killer's mine?"

"Like we said—what are the odds the bodies were buried on top of it—so close to the support structure? Our killer knew this place."

Forester studied her, considered this comment, then nodded once and began to clamber into the dark, moldy hole in the ground.

"Wait! Forester—wait! What are you doing?"

"Investigating. That's what the little 'I' stands for in FBI."

"Hang on—shouldn't we wait until—"

"The professionals show up?" Forest glanced at her, already with his legs dangling into the unknown darkness. He looked completely unperturbed by the situation. Excited even. He winked at her. "That's us, Checkers. We're the professionals. Well... When did you start training again?"

"Next week!" she squeaked.

"Ah, shucks—consider this an object lesson. Come on!"

And he slipped into the darkness, without so much as a flicker of hesitation, leaving Artemis standing in the woods, very much averse to the idea of even dipping a toe in that horrible shadow. She took a tentative step closer, peering into the dark. She could just make out the form of Cameron, where he moved about. She also spotted other things moving through the disheveled moss and crawling over the rotting forest floor.

Spiders as large as her thumb. A centipede scurried out of sight, hiding beneath a small rock, only a foot away from her.

She wasn't proud of it, but Artemis yelped, taking a quick step to the side.

Now, as prickles crawled down her spine, she couldn't help but pat at her back, fidgeting, and twisting with jerking motions. Artemis did not wear a suit. She didn't believe in them. Instead, she wore a comfortable, baggy shirt. Longsleeved. And slacks.

Instead of perfume, she smelled of soap.

She valued cleanliness, hygiene. Clearly, this passion was not shared by the insufferable man who had just dropped through a crater in the forest floor.

This very same man was no longer speaking to her. She could hear movement below, but no comments.

Tentatively, resenting him deeply for forcing this, she called out, "Are you all right?"

He didn't reply.

"Forester?"

Still no response.

She glared into the dark. "That's not funny, Cameron. If you can hear me, you better reply."

He said nothing. She could still see the shadow moving, though.

She bit her lip.

This, she decided, was the grand difference between the two of them. Forester was the sort to live by a motto of: Ready, Fire, Aim.

Artemis on the other hand didn't even know how to disengage the safety on a weapon. Firearm training was the part of her upcoming tutelage—as an official FBI consultant—that she was least looking forward to.

But also obstacle courses... and mud. She'd heard mud was involved on FBI training grounds. As much as she enjoyed facing a problem, studying it, reaching a solution, she *hated* this part. The spiders, the mud, the mold, the darkness, the bundles of bodies back up the cliff... It all bothered her immensely.

But now she stood alone in the woods. Forester wasn't replying. And so, with a frustrated sigh, she took a quick step towards the hole, like ripping a band-aid. Her intention had been to lower herself, swing her legs in, then—using a root for a handhold—to deposit herself slowly into the dark, following Forester.

What happened instead, though, was as she took a step, more of the forest floor gave out under her, and she fell into the dark with a desperate shout.

CHAPTER 5

Artemis' shout cut short as Agent Forester caught her tumbling form. Her body jolted, protesting the sudden stop.

"Nice of you to drop in, Checkers," Forester muttered.

She exhaled quickly, spitting dust and pushing against Forester's form. His calloused hands were under her arms, one half wrapped awkwardly around her back, her chest pressed to his where he'd used his own frame to help catch her.

He slowly lowered her to the ground, but she pushed away. "You did that on purpose!" she snapped.

"Did what?"

"You knew I'd be concerned, so you didn't say anything!"

"And you say you're not psychic. But keep it down—don't want to cause a cave-in."

Artemis held back another retort, blinking once, then swallowing slowly. She paused long enough to spit more dust. "A cave-in?" she murmured. "That's... a possibility?"

"Dunno. Look there."

Forester's flashlight app on his phone now flickered through the dark, illuminating the rest of the pit. Indeed, Artemis realized they'd discovered the mineshaft. Old, wooden supports upheld criss-crossing over-arching beams. The wood was well beyond use, and portions of the muddy walls were crumbling.

The ground itself was strewn with puddles where water had turned stagnant. Artemis wrinkled her nose, trying desperately not to breathe in too deeply.

"Gross," she murmured.

Forester meanwhile was stepping in one of those puddles to reach the other side of the entrance. He moved with a slow, carefree gait, shining his light around as if on some sightseeing tour.

"M-maybe we should go back," Artemis said quietly.

He shot a glance back at her, grinning in the dark, his lupine smirk illuminated by the bright light. "Scared, huh?"

"N-no," she snapped. "Just... maybe we should go back," she repeated, more firmly. She shot a look towards the opening in the ceiling which was still discarding stray leaves, allowing them to flutter towards the muddy floor.

Forester watched a leaf land in another puddle, shot a look at Artemis, shrugged, then said, "Suit yourself."

Promptly, he turned and began moving back up the tunnel, away from her once more. Artemis scowled after him, considering the wisdom of grabbing a big fistful of mud and launching it at those wide shoulders.

But then she sighed, caught herself to avoid inhaling too much in the way of stale air, and fell into step. Instead of moving through the puddles, she skirted the wall, shoulders scraping stones free, and then—shoes mercifully dry—followed hastily after the big man.

"Where are we going?" she whispered.

"Dunno," he shot back. "Investigating. Remember."

"It's... it's... what if..."

"The killer is down here, waiting for us in the dark?"

Artemis blinked. "No... I was going to ask what if we breathe in toxic mold. But your hypothetical is *far* worse."

Forester looked back at her, frowning deeply. "Huh. Toxic mold. Don't like the sound of that."

Artemis meanwhile was busy jumping at every shadow created by Forester's bright light. She tried not to react at a sudden flicker of her own shadow, but it was a close thing.

She missed her laptop. Missed the protection of a locked door and an internet connection. Chess was far more sanitary, far safer. This... this business of stomping through mud puddles was *not* her idea of a good time.

Still, she'd come back to Pinelake to find Helen, hadn't she? To find out, once and for all, with certainty, what had happened. And also to put a stop to whatever her father was cooking up in that prison of his.

If she had to get her hands... and feet... a bit dirty...

She swallowed.

She'd have to learn how.

And so, forcing herself to breathe slowly, she continued after Forester, following him through the dark. A couple of times the lanky man paused, glancing in the dark, and scanning the floor.

The deeper they went, the lower the ceiling became. Eventually, Forester had to duck his head, his shoulders nearly scraping against the ceiling.

One of these times, as he paused to scan some discovered item, he pulled up short. "Look at that."

Artemis didn't want to look at anything. Artemis wanted to turn on her heel and run.

But she supposed this wasn't an option. And so, with a sigh, she peered at the indicated item, bending, elbows resting on her knees.

And then she realized what it was.

A coil of rope.

Only one problem.

It wasn't frayed, old, worn rope, but new, clean material, spooled on the ground like a coiled snake.

"Climbing gear," Forester said with a nod.

"Maybe we should get backup," Artemis whispered.

"I am the backup," Forester muttered. "Honestly, Checkers, sometimes I wonder about you."

"Well, please don't. The less time I spend in your brain the better for both of us."

"You can say that again. Careful, dead rat."

Of course, he had waited until she had stepped on.10 the carcass to say anything.

She yelped, jerking her foot back, and trying to kick, in the same motion, the horrible, rotting thing towards agent Forester.

She missed, though, and he was moving again heading deeper into the dark.

So far, there had been no branching paths. But now, the light from Cameron's phone illuminated a Y. The right branching path was blocked, by boulders and stones, and tons of mud.

"Tunnel collapsed," Forester whispered.

"I can see that. What's that? No, that. Not your foot, genius, that metal case your light keeps catching."

Finally, the spotlight from Forester's phone found what she was indicating.

They both went still.

A metal chest down the left side of the branching hall.

They stared at it. Artemis instantly wanted to turn and run.

Forester was shaking his head slowly, murmuring, "Nothing good will come of looking in that... We should check it out."

This time she actually tried to grab his arm, but he pulled free, marching directly towards the item.

He paused by the metal chest, frowning slowly. Then, with a quick, excited look back towards Artemis involving a quick wiggle of his eyebrows—he grabbed the lid and tried to fling it open.

It was locked.

He scowled, glanced at the padlock securing the thing, reached for his weapon, aimed and fired twice.

The lock spun, then shattered.

Forester waited for the metal to cool a few seconds, then lifted the shattered lock, tossing it off to the side. With a final glance back at Artemis, he reached down and flung open the lid.

A cloud of dust erupted, and he gasped, choking at the ground, shaking his head and trying to hold back a sneeze with the back of his forefinger. As his other hand wanded the air, clearing the particles, Artemis tentatively approached.

The two of them peered into the open chest, frowning.

Mention of the gold mine had brought to mind memories of Artemis' first case. The only woman who'd ever given Artemis a hug—Mrs. Kramer—had been killed by her husband. She'd also been buried on a pile of gold.

But now, staring into the open chest, Artemis shivered, swallowing back a horrible shout.

Holes were punctured in the metal from the opposite side. She hadn't seen these at first. There, laying on a small, ratty blanket, a woman was curled, motionless. She had dark hair resting across pale features. One hand curled under her chin, resting motionless.

Her feet wedged against the base of the metal. She wore a thin t-shirt and frayed sweatpants. She smelled of sweat and worse.

"Is she... Is she dead?" Artemis whispered.

Forester leaned in, peering at the woman. His fingers leapt out, moving towards her neck in search of a pulse. The moment he touched her skin, though, she yelped, jerking upright and staring. Her eyes carried a haunted look. She trembled horribly, causing the lid of her metal coffin to rattle. She leaned back on the rusted hinges, eyes darting madly between the two of them.

"He says hello," she whispered after a moment.

Her voice was rasping, strained, clearly parched. She licked her cracked and dry lips, attempting to wet them, and forced a quick, giggling laugh. "He says hello," she whispered more fiercely. "He says it! He says it! He said hello!"

She was laughing now, shaking, her shoulders trembling horribly. And then, she began to cry, dipping her head, tears streaking her cheeks and cutting through her grimy face, leaving clean trails of weathered skin.

"Ma'am," Artemis said, moving past her initial terror, "Are you alright? Ma'am, can you hear me?"

The woman was shaking her head, whispering to herself now. Artemis tried to reach out, touching the woman's shoulder with a gentle tap. The moment Artemis' fingers touched the woman, she went stiff, staring like a startled doe.

"P-please," The woman whispered. "He'll be back soon. You need to help me. P-please help me!" She was stammering so badly now that she paused to console herself, shaking her head furiously.

Artemis just stared at Forester, completely stunned and at a loss for words.

Agent Forester was glancing down the long hall. "Who did this to you? Is he here?"

The woman just shook her head, and as she did, Artemis noticed her dark hair had waves at the end. Curling hair. She hesitated, peering at the grimy face, wondering if perhaps she recognized this woman. With a hesitant, jolting voice, Artemis whispered, "What's your name?"

She dreaded the answer.

The woman blinked, then said, "Sierra... I... I'm Sierra."

Artemis let out a sigh bordering relief. Part of her wondered at this reaction. Didn't she want to find Helen?

But another part of her realized the truth. If Helen *was* still alive, did that mean she'd been kept by some horrible kidnapper for the last seventeen years, locked away? Locked in a metal chest with breathing holes?

The woman in the box, though, was trembling again. Her eyes rolled back. She murmured, a final time, "He w-wants to say... h-hello..." And then she slumped over, motionless.

Artemis stared at the woman in the metal box, heart hammering.

Forester was already pulling a radio, pressing the transceiver and barking, "Wade—hey, asshole, turn on your—yeah, there. Listen, found something. Send six, stretcher, call paras. Hurry! Coordinates coming. Head about fifty feet south of that, big ol' hole. If you miss it, you're a prick. Got it?"

A heavy, static-filled sigh on the other end. But it was a credit to Wade's special forces training that he made no protest. He simply said, "Got it. Coming."

Forester lowered the radio, glancing back at the woman in the metal case.

"How long do you think she's been in there?" Artemis whispered.

"No water. No food. Not long. I smell piss... not shit. Not long."

Artemis felt her stomach sour, but she resisted the urge to turn away. Forester was busy checking along the edge of the metal box. And then he shot a look down the remainder of the mineshaft. He glanced at the ceiling, frowning.

"Think our bones are up there somewhere?"

"I don't know," Artemis whispered. "B-but... I think we have more bodies, Forester."

"Hmm?"

"There."

He followed her trembling finger.

The light flared down the remainder of the tunnel. It cut off after about fifty feet, blockaded by another collapsed beam. But there, wedged against the collapsed portion of the mine shaft...

Artemis stumbled back this time, holding back a sudden yelp of terror.

Bones.

Pale, bleached, white bones.

Old bones.

A third mass burial site.

And this one, by the looks of things, was larger than the others. Piles of human bones rested in the back of the tunnel, completely picked clean by age, bacteria and the occasional critter that had found its way into the tunnel.

She knew some of the critters by *their* skeletons. Someone had killed the scavengers just as quickly as the humans. Smaller, animal skeletons littered the edges of the cave as Artemis and Forester stared in horrified awe at the grisly spectacle.

The woman in the metal case was still breathing shallowly, and so Artemis forced her gaze away from this newest burial site.

This wasn't just a serial killer...

This... this felt like something else.

Something far darker, far worse. She'd never heard of so many victims before. Already, they'd discovered nearly twenty above ground. But here... she was no expert, but a cursory glance told her there were at least another twenty, maybe more down in the tunnel.

Almost forty victims... Spanning twenty years.

The chances that Helen Blythe was among the slain had suddenly skyrocketed.

Artemis felt her own hands trembling now. She couldn't, however, shake the horror confronting her. The woman in the metal chest hinted at another grave truth.

This killer, whoever he was, was still active. Still very much alive... and still very much on the hunt.

"Wade, dammit, hurry up," Forester was barking into his radio again. "We have a woman here. She's unconscious. Get paramedics down here fast. Kick their slow asses if you have to. Hurry!"

Artemis didn't know what to do. She just stood dazed, staring at the woman in the metal chest.

He wants to say hello.

What did that mean?

Artemis found her stomach tightening in knots, though. As she considered this question, the tightening of her stomach only exacerbated.

Panic was setting in.

Forester shot her a quick look, frowning. "Breathe," he murmured slowly. He was tapping a hand in a steady rhythm against his leg now. "Blythe, it's going to be fine. *Breathe.*"

She remembered Forester mentioning that his mother used to have panic attacks. She tried to smile, tried to nod, but all she could think about was the rising anxiety, the tightening in her gut, and the horror of a bone-filled tunnel.

And then she collapsed to the ground, shaking, stomach tight, eyes sealed shut if only to block out the horrible scene.

He wants to say hello.

What... *in the hell...* did that mean?

CHAPTER 6

Artemis woke in the back of an ambulance, inhaling something pungent. Her eyes fluttered, and her stomach tightened as she tried to sit up. She blinked rapidly and realized a familiar face was holding something under her nose.

"There we are," said the ever-cheerful voice of Dr. Bryant. The middle-aged coroner was beaming down at Artemis and waving a hand under her nose as if to clear the air.

Artemis inhaled and winced at another sharp odor.

"Just clearing the sinuses dear," said Dr. Bryant, patting Artemis on the cheek with an open hand, which Artemis desperately hoped wasn't still wearing the glove used to tend to the corpses.

As Artemis sat upright, partly groggy and partly with a lancing pain in her head, she glanced across a wooded space towards the side of a gray road circled by a metal banister. Somewhere in the distance, Artemis thought she heard the authoritative voice of Agent Grant calling out orders.

Her attention lingered on this loud voice, but Dr. Bryant's waving hand returned Artemis' focus to the more immediate surroundings.

She was inside an ambulance, leaning against the side metal wall. Behind her, she heard movements, commotion.

Artemis winced, trying to turn, but Dr. Bryant caught her chin. "No, child—wait. No sudden movements. Hmm, you had quite a scare back there. I'm so sorry, dear."

Artemis blinked, glancing at the older woman, frowning briefly. She wiped the scowl from her features a second later though, and flashed a quick smile followed by a nod. "Thank you," she murmured. She studied Miracle, wondering how much of the woman was a performance and how much was personality.

It seemed an odd thing to have so much... character jammed into one compact body. But the woman's sparkly earrings and rainbow-pony t-shirt were secondary to the warm smile creasing her lips. For a brief moment, staring at the coroner, Artemis was reminded of Mrs. Kramer... She'd called the woman *Aunt*, after all.

Now, though, she shook her head, trying to clear her mind and refocus. It took her a few seconds to realize what had happened.

But as the memory returned, she stiffened, her heart hammering horribly. She stared at Dr. Bryant. "Oh...oh, no," she murmured.

"Yes, dear?"

Artemis swallowed, massaging her head, closing her eyes. The scent of the forest mingled with the odor of exhaust coming from the idling ambulance and many of the other vehicles lining the road. A few angry brake lights glared at her from where other vehicles had recently pulled along the mountain road.

"The... the bodies," Artemis whispered. "We—we found..."

"Yes, yes I heard. My assistant is going through it right now. They'll be digging through the night, I imagine. The journey to the mineshaft, I'm afraid, would be just a bit too much on my ankles." She chuckled at this and gave an airy little wave of her fingers.

Artemis tried to return the smile but it didn't quite work. Then, she remembered the rest of it. That poor woman trapped in the metal coffin. The scent of the mildew. And those strange words.

He wants to say hello...

"Where is she?" Artemis whispered. "Where..."

"Hmm? Oh—the woman you found. Right behind you, dear. Only the one ambulance currently, I'm afraid."

"Dr. Bryant!" A voice called from behind them. "We need to get going. She's low on fluids. We don't have the right IV."

Miracle sighed, but it wasn't a frustrated sigh. Artemis wondered if the kindly coroner *knew* how to get frustrated. Instead, the woman with the brightly colored hair nodded towards the person who'd spoken from the back seat. "Alright, Sean. Ms. Blythe, would you like to go to the hospit—oh, I guess not."

Artemis was already pushing from the back of the ambulance, her legs somewhat wobbly as she stepped back onto the asphalt road. She turned, glancing into the back of the ambulance finally, twisting to witness the woman they'd found secured under a blanket on a stretcher. The woman was motionless, and it took Artemis a horrifying second to see if she was even breathing.

But when Artemis spotted the faint rise and fall of the woman's chest, she let out a quick sigh of relief.

"She's alive?" Artemis said.

"Yes, dear."

The two paramedics in the back of the ambulance were still busy connecting something to Sierra's arm. That was the name she'd given. Sierra.

Not Helen.

As Artemis stared at the poor woman, she went still. "Um m... wait!" she said sharply.

One of the paramedics had been reaching for the doors to close them. At her comment, the woman gave a quick shake of her head. "Sorry, lady, but we really need to get—"

"No—please. What's *that*!" Artemis pointed sharply.

The woman hesitated, glancing back. The other coroner, a young man, glanced where she was pointing.

"What is that, Sean?" Dr. Bryant asked.

Sean hesitated, wrinkling his nose. He lowered something he'd been attempting to insert, unsuccessfully, into the victim's arm. He unstrapped a rubber band around her wrist, and then pulled the woman's sleeve back.

"Huh," the two paramedics said, mirroring each other.

Dr. Bryant leaned in as well, staring at the tattoo.

An inky set of numbers were tattooed into Sierra's left arm. Ten digits, including the area code. A phone number in ink, indelibly etched into the woman's arm. A phone number like what one might place on a dog's nametag—an owner claiming its pet.

But also...

He wants to say hello.

Artemis felt a faint shiver at these words.

"We can take a picture if you want," the young paramedic called urgently, "but we need to go. She's not doing well."

Dr. Bryant nodded quickly. "Take a photo and send it to Ms. Blythe here. Now go!"

But Artemis was already turning quickly, looking for Forester. "No photo needed," she muttered. She'd already committed the ten digits to memory. As she moved away from the stationary ambulance, picking up her pace, she gave a faint fluttering farewell wave with her left hand at Dr. Bryant. But she was too distracted to offer much more than that.

Where the hell was Forester?

She thought she spotted Agent Grant down the side of the road, near one of the larger trees where the bodies had been found. She couldn't make out what the pale-haired supervising agent was saying, but Artemis scanned past her, looking for the woman's nephew. Where was Forester?

When she didn't spot him, she sighed, surmising he must have been the one to bring her back to the ambulance and then returned to the new burial site.

Artemis felt confident they'd have the good sense to brush that metal chest for fingerprints along with that fresh rope they'd discovered near Sierra.

She shot a quick look back towards the retreating ambulance, witnessing as it curved up the switchback, leaving rubber against the road.

But then, frowning to herself, Artemis reached a decision. No sign of Forester...

He wants to say Hello.

Was she right?

Whose number was tattooed on Sierra? The ambulance was gone. Artemis stood on the side of the road, very much alone for the moment. She sighed slowly and then lifted her phone, entering the ten digits from memory, and frowning with each digit entered.

Then, briefly, she stared at the glowing screen beneath the overhanging branches of the bristling firs around. The shadows of the mountain, the fading afternoon light cast the slopes in a strange gloom.

Artemis stared at her phone a second longer, feeling the faint nip of chill wind coming over the slopes. And then, with a determined nod to herself, she lifted the phone, listening to it ring.

It didn't even complete the first full sound.

The moment she called, a voice answered.

"Greetings, Artemis Blythe," it said, "This *is* a surprise. I had been hoping to speak to you, but not under these auspices." The voice went quiet, waiting politely.

It sounded as if it was using some sort of voice scrambler that made it shift between high and low pitches, like whistling steam from an old-fashioned teapot. Or like the musical notes of some great symphony. There was an ethereal, otherworldly quality to the musical voice.

And the moment it had spoken her name, she felt a terrible shiver along her back. "D-do I know you?" she said slowly, looking around now, searching the nearest branches. She knew smoke and mirrors.

By calling her name out, he'd wanted to sound impressive. But she wasn't a mark. She wasn't a sheep. Information like that only narrowed possibilities. She wasn't impressed, she was clued in.

If he knew who was speaking to him, he either recognized her number, had managed to look it up as she'd called or was watching her that very moment. It was her turn to fish for information. So she said, more firmly, "Do I know you?"

"No, Artemis, I don't believe so. I'm a friend of your father's. You haven't been very kind to your father, have you? You should respect your parents. It's one of the Ten Commandments, you know?" That strange, pitch-changing, auto-tuned, musical voice was causing an itch in her ear.

She didn't respond right away, processing the information quickly. Her eyes were still searching the forest canopy. A friend of her father's? A quick online search could have helped him speak like this... but the idea that she hadn't been very kind to her father? Very similar words to what her old man had used back at that prison.

So that meant he *did* know who she was. It wasn't conclusive but it gave her a working theory. Sometimes, all a chess player had to work off was theories.

Which meant, when she'd called, he'd seen her. Narrowing options further.

Only two, in fact.

He was either watching her from the woods...

Which was why she'd been scanning the trees. But no one was watching. She'd even stepped a few paces back behind one of the vehicles to disturb line of sight.

So there was another option.

The killer was keeping track some other way... had seen her... was tracking... The only solution: a camera.

And, after a few more moments of scanning the canopy, she spotted it.

She didn't stare at it long, preferring to keep the information she had under wraps. One could never be sure what advantage information would provide. But there'd been a glint in the branches of a tree behind one of the light posts near the very same switchback where the ambulance had disappeared.

The man on the phone was watching her.

As her mind moved through these analytical steps, it helped dissuade a rising temptation to fear. She swallowed slowly. "I have some friends who I think would like to speak with you..."

"No, thank you, Artemis. I see you spotted my camera."

Now, she did hesitate. He was observant. Quick. Not good. She said, slowly, "Why was your number tattooed on a friend of mine?"

"Sierra? She's my friend, not yours, Artemis. Keep that straight, please, or we're done here."

Jockeying for position. Just like her father might. She opened her mouth to reply, but he cut in, another consistent move with someone attempting to control the conversation. But his next words only increased her concern.

"I'm not attempting to... what would your father call it, *jockey for position*? Hmm? Oh—I see I surprised you there. Well, dear, don't worry about that. I wanted to say hello for a very simple reason. It has been...." A long sigh, a deep, shaky inhale with more lilting notes. "A very, very long time that I've enjoyed my small grove. But now it looks as if I'll be moving. I knew this was coming. When they decided to burn my woods." A faint sound like smacking lips. Artemis was doing her best to pay attention to every sound, every hint. She didn't need a recording device, though she wished she'd had one.

But the sounds, the inflections, the background noise—of which there was very little—were all committed to memory.

"Yes, I knew it was coming. Twenty-five years, little Artemis," he said quietly. "Twenty-five years, I've enjoyed my playthings... but now, alas," he gave a dramatic sigh, "I must bid adieu."

"Who are you?" she shot back.

"That would be telling."

"You say you know my father?"

A genuinely amused chuckle. "You could say that."

"Is my father behind this? You're saying you killed these women? Did my father tell you to?"

The voice went suddenly cold, and Artemis could practically feel her arms frost.

"*I* was moving in the shadows *long* before second-rate charlatans, *Ms. Blythe.* Do *not* compare me to your father again, or you and I will have a date with my tools."

She felt another clot in her stomach forming, but now, at the bottom of the slope, she spotted Agent Forester trudging back up the slope. She stepped once more behind the parked van, hiding her arm, and then, desperately, she began waving and gesturing, trying her best to catch Cameron's attention.

But he had paused to speak with his aunt. More accurately, he had come to a halt to listen as Agent Grant tongue-lashed her nephew. This, Artemis had determined, was a favorite past-time of the sophisticated, no-nonsense woman.

Now, though, Forester took some time to lip-off, as he so often did. The back and forth between aunt and nephew was like a sarcastic and somewhat cynical tennis match.

But now, as Artemis tried to wave at Forester, she kept speaking if only to keep the man on the line. "You're saying you killed all of these women, then?"

"Hmm. Yes."

"Almost forty bodies... is that right?"

Another cold tone. Almost as if he was offended. "Sixty-five, Ms. Blythe. Look harder. I didn't keep all my playthings in the same place."

Sixty-five dead?

She swallowed a sudden lump in her throat as if the airways had closed. She shook her head in disbelief, still clasping the phone to the side of her face. Sixty-five... she'd never heard of a more prolific serial killer in North America.

Perhaps she hadn't *wanted* to hear... but sixty-five? Her own father had killed seven... Though this was a disputed number if he was telling the truth about Helen... or not.

Artemis shivered. She wondered if she ought to ask the man on the phone. Part of her wondered if he knew what she was thinking. This had always been the tactic her father used. Digging *certain* information in order to appear omniscient to allow the other person to then fill in the blanks.

But as the silence stretched, she determined the man on the phone didn't know what she wanted to ask. Instead, he said, "This is a courtesy call, Ms. Blythe. Now, I want you to listen closely. Can you do that?"

Forester was looking at her now, frowning up the slope. Artemis was listening but still gesturing wildly. When she realized Cameron was peering in her direction she began to gesture even more insistently, eyes widening every now and then like punctuation.

Forester held a finger up to Grant, silencing her. She slapped the finger out of her face. Forester broke into a jog, hastening towards Artemis.

CHAPTER 7

As he drew nearer, Artemis said, louder, so he could hear, "I'm listening closely. You still haven't given me a name."

"What's wrong?" Forester called out, but Artemis' finger—still hidden from the camera by the van—darted to her lips. Forester went quiet, frowning now. Then, because it was Cameron, instead of doing as he was told, he tried again, louder. "Who are you talking to?"

"Ah," said the voice on the other line. "Is that Agent Cameron Forester? I can't say I know him very well. But I do know you, Ms. Blythe, and I know your associates. Invite him over. Perhaps he'd enjoy our game."

"Who are you?" She said, insisting the question again.

A chuckle this time. A mercurial fellow, this. Serial killer or something else? His number had been tattooed on the woman in the mineshaft. Near the bodies. Near the mass graves...

He had to be the killer. It was the only thing that made sense.

As she felt this conclusion settle, she also felt a cold chill. She swallowed slowly, frowning as he answered her question with a snort. "Inconsequential things, names. You can call me Professor."

"Why? Are you a professor?"

"That would be on the nose, wouldn't it?"

Artemis had turned her phone on speaker now, and Forester had come to a halt next to her, wide-eyed, listening. Agent Grant was moving towards them now too, scowling as she approached, but as she spotted their expressions her scowl turned into something closer to a look of concern. She picked up her pace, moving hastily through the leaves. Artemis realized Grant had two, elegant high heels clutched in one hand, thrown over her shoulder, and—indifferent to those watching—she marched barefoot through the leaves, moving towards them. She wore a dress, as well, suggesting she'd been at some event or other. Two emerald earrings swished from her ears, framing her neat, tidy hair-do which was pulled up with only the use of a single hairpin.

Artemis looked back at the phone. "Alright, Professor," she said slowly, "Do you have a name?"

Forester was busy trying to mime something to her, but Artemis gave a quick shake of her head, glancing off towards the camera. Forester followed her gaze, frowned, then shook his head.

She mouthed the word, behind the van, *Camera.*

Forester's eyebrows went high. He mimed with his finger, shielding it with his body, a rolling motion. *Keep him talking.* Forester's own phone was in his off hand, and he was hastily texting something to someone. Likely another agent.

The chances of tracking this call were far outside Artemis' wheelhouse. But in the movies, people always tried to stall the bad guy on the phone. So she waited patiently as she received another tongue-lashing for her question.

"Don't be silly, Ms. Blythe. Please, pay attention now. No more business about names. That's the game. I've played this game for nearly three decades. But you, and those on Forester's little team, didn't know they were playing. And losing. One other thing... that mineshaft is *not* from a gold mine. I heard the speculation earlier. It was a mineshaft to nowhere. No gold was found. Nearly six hundred thousand dollars was spent on building this big old badger burrow. At the time, nearly a hundred and fifty years ago, that was a lot of money, Ms. Blythe."

Artemis frowned to herself. "So this isn't a gold mineshaft."

"It is an empty husk. A worthless tribute to the vanity of man. Nothing accomplished, nothing earned, just wasted time... And so are you listening now? You too Cameron."

"Hi there," Forester said, still typing furiously on his phone.

"I don't know you as well Mr. Forester, so please do keep quiet while I speak to your intellectual superior."

"Ouch," Forester said.

The voice suddenly raged. One moment attempting to communicate control, calm. The next, furious as a storm. The screech of the lilting voice scrambler increased in pitch, and Artemis had to hold her phone further away, grimacing. "Shut your bastard mouth, you worthless little waste of placenta! I will take your bloody eyes!"

Forester blinked, scratching at his chin. "Was it something I said?" he asked.

Artemis cut in quickly, anticipating another tirade. "Professor," she said, trying to keep polite, "please don't mind Forester. What is it you want to tell me?"

A deep exhale, inhale, exhale... A long pause. A faint swallow. Forester had a mean look in his eyes as if he was gearing up to say something else nasty. But Artemis didn't believe this would be productive. So she quickly cut in. Instead of shaking her head or trying to verbally silence him, she stepped forward, elbowing Forester in the ribs.

He winced, letting out a puff of air.

Then, Artemis lifted her phone again, waiting patiently.

The man on the line, sufficiently calm now, murmured, "Tell Agent Forester that if he tests me, I *will* rise to the challenge. Understand?"

"He didn't mean anything," Artemis said. She glanced at Forester, who was no longer texting but had raised his own phone, flashing her a message.

The text simply read, *two minutes. Keep him on.*

She nodded once. The man on the other line, oblivious, was saying, "Pay attention. I have three new toys. They're as empty as this tunnel of ours. But they're still alive. Are we clear?"

Forester went suddenly still, any wise-ass remark dying on his lips. Artemis said, shakily, "Three new toys?"

"Yes, Ms. Blythe. Keep up. These cretins aren't like us, but if you keep spouting inanity I may lose all respect for you. And facing Radesh so soon? Tsk. Tsk." he tutted, then said, "Three new toys. Breathing... for now. All of them very much like Sierra."

"Does Sierra have a last name?"

"That's not my part of the game. I've already played my part. I've left you three presents. Three of them missing. Would you like a clue, or would you prefer the challenge of figuring it out yourself?"

"Hang on," Artemis said swiftly. "This isn't a game..." She trailed off, though, catching herself.

"You do know who you're speaking to, don't you?"

"I don't. I've never heard of anyone known only as the Professor."

"That isn't what I mean. I mean to say, your version of reasoning with me would have involved playing on my compassion. I assure you, there is none of that. I've never tasted it. Not as a child. Not now."

"How old are you?"

A little tinkling laugh. "Good—good, you are *playing* now! There we are. So clue or not?"

"Yes!" Artemis said desperately.

He sounded disappointed that she said this. He sighed, though, and said, "Well, as you wish. The first toy was empty of her heart. The second toy was empty of a brain. And the third toy was empty of a soul. Good luck."

And he hung up.

Artemis stood behind the van, phone clutched in her hand, staring wide-eyed at the device. Forester cursed, studying his own phone. "Techie missed it," he said, then spat off to the side. "Holy shit. What was that Checkers?"

"I... I think he's the killer," Artemis murmured. She stared at Forester. "He said he's killed sixty-five victims..."

"What did you say?" Agent Grant's voice cut in as she reached them now, too. Her bare feet were stained with leaves and had some foliage stuck against the side of her foot. Even the way she stood, barefoot on the side of a murder scene, her dress smooth and sleek, her high-heels resting near her shoulder where she held them aloft, angled back somewhat like a rain jacket thrown over her shoulder—all of it somehow communicated elegance and indifference.

Her tone, though, was severe. "What did you just say, Ms. Blythe?"

Artemis shook her head, mind-reeling. "I... he seemed to know my name. Or else he was researching me. There's a camera over there, see—by the light post. It has audio. He heard us speaking about the gold mine. He says it isn't that. He says he's killed sixty-five people." Artemis rattled off the information rapidly then went quiet, watching Agent Grant.

The older woman scowled, crossing her arms, glancing to Forester then back to Artemis. "Sixty-five? Did we get a number?"

"Burner," Forester said with a snort. "An old pay-as-you-go flip-phone." He was still reading the updating texts which vibrated his own device every few seconds.

Grant was frowning now at Artemis. "What else did he say?"

"He says he has three more victims. Alive. But locked away. Probably in some horrible, metal coffin like Sierra was."

"The name of our survivor," Forester added helpfully.

Grant nodded. "Three? Anything else?" She paused and held up a finger, silencing any response in order to call out, "Wade, come here please!" Then she glanced at Artemis, bobbing her head once, a single strand of pale hair falling past her eyes.

"Umm... he said," Artemis paused, frowning, "A few things. But..." She hesitated, reaching back into her mind, searching for the exact phrasing, and then she recited, "*The first toy was empty of her heart. The second toy was empty of a brain. And the third toy was empty of a soul.*"

67

"Was?" Forester said. "Why *was*? Did he already kill them?"

"I... I don't know," Artemis said, her voice shaking. "It didn't sound like it. But maybe... he did leave Sierra alive, though."

"How did you get his number?" Forester demanded.

"A tattoo on our survivor's arm. She was marked like cattle."

"Shit."

"Yes," Artemis agreed.

"We don't know this is our killer," Agent Grant said. "We don't even know if these corpses *were* killed. For all we know he exhumed them from graveyards and buried them here."

"Really?" Forester said. "That's your theory?"

"No. That's unlikely but possible. He's taunting us. A camera? A phone call? Why now? Hmm? I spoke with Dr. Bryant. One of those corpses is at least twenty years old."

"Twenty-five according to the Professor," Artemis supplied.

"According to who?"

"The... umm, that's what he called himself."

"Wonderful. Twenty-five, then. My point being, why now? How did he know we would find the girl? Why was he waiting for a call?"

"He said he was expecting us after the forest was burned," Artemis said. "Said he knew it would bring us calling."

"Makes sense," Forester murmured. "This place was thick with undergrowth, but now..." he waved along the road. "Enough people come through here, it was inevitable they'd find the spot eventually."

"But why *today*?" Grant asked. "The survivor... how did he know we'd find her *today*."

Artemis cleared her throat, hesitated, then murmured, "I don't think he did."

Both the agents looked at her. She sighed slowly, closed her eyes but opened them again. "Feigning omniscience. It's a narcissist's tactic. But..." She bit her lip. "I don't think he knew *when* we'd discover his little cave. He seemed surprised... almost excited that I was on the line."

"He *knew* you'd be on the line?"

"N-no... Ummm... Not to be weird, but I'm a bit of a celebrity among the creeps and weirdos in this region," Artemis said, wincing. "My father was..." she swallowed, "something of a celebrity as well. As his daughter, I was in the limelight for a bit. A lot of articles, a lot of news stories. It just sort of... caught on..." She stared at the ground as she said this part, then sighed and looked up with a shrug. "Anyway... I don't think he knew that I was going to be here at all. I think he was surprised to see me. But I *do* think he was expecting *someone,* like our camper who found the first spot, to discover his hiding spots. He knew it was a matter of time with the controlled burn."

"That doesn't explain how he knew our survivor would live long enough to deliver that phone number."

But Forester was scowling now. He looked downright furious. She had seen him like this before. Often when young women of a certain age were involved. She'd had glimpses... just glimpses... that specific *types* of victims reminded him of someone he'd once been close to. "Because," Forester murmured. "She's right... He *didn't* know she would still be alive. A few of the newer bodies," he said slowly, waving a hand towards the first tree they'd found, "were very old. But some were fresh."

Suddenly Agent Grant seemed to realize what they were hinting at. "Oh..." she said softly. Her lips pressed in a small, severe line.

Oh indeed.

The killer didn't care if Sierra delivered his message. Or one of the other victims did. She wondered how many women had been locked in that mineshaft, slowly dying... And then, if left undiscovered, dumped and replaced by a new... *toy*.

A bolt of absolute hatred lanced through her. She forgot about Helen for a second. Forgot about the two agents.

That sing-song, self-aggrandizing voice... it made her want to puke. He had killed *scores* of people. It didn't seem right he could only spend one lifetime in prison.

She'd already decided what type of person the Professor was. Perhaps it was the recent visit with her father. Or that the Ghost-killer's name had been brought up in conversation. Or just the sheer evil of what was buried in the side of the mountain...

But Artemis *very much* wanted to be present when this particular hound was caught. In fact, if she could, she wanted to be the one to help do it.

CHAPTER 8

The Professor lowered his phone, listening to the faint tapping sound behind him. He reached up, wiping saliva from his chin. Sometimes, he allowed his emotions to get the better of him. He slowly lowered his hand, wiping his fingers off on the cloth next to him. A few flecks of red stained that cloth, and he frowned, determined to clean up better next time.

The tapping behind him grew more insistent.

He lowered the phone, allowing it to fall into a small jar of acid. Royal water. One of the strongest acids in the world. Used for parting gold from foreign matter. He'd always been somewhat obsessed with gold.

Finding value in otherwise worthless things.

Many times... he would *search* for value in shiny, glinting vessels only to find them empty and coarse. He frowned at the thought, glaring at his hand.

"Did you hear that?" he called over his shoulder.

More insistent tapping. A faint, desperate scream. Muffled, though. He shook his head. And sighed, moving away from his workbench.

There were other jars of acid on the table. Some of them were in use, separating the most recent of his prospected material, while others were dormant. He stopped by the table, leaning over and lifting the sharp pick. He gave it a couple of small swings, chuckling to himself.

A silly thing with which to pry open empty vessels... A toy, really. But the Professor had seen value in its use, all those years ago. And so he kept to the tradition of it. Traditions mattered after all.

He lifted the pick and turned to face the metal storage container. "Coming, coming," he called. "Don't panic. I only put you in a few minutes ago. I told you to hold your breath!"

He approached, whistling. Air tight—sealed. By now, she was drawing on stale air. The real threat of being trapped in a box like that *was not* lack of oxygen, but rather carbon dioxide poisoning. "Stop screaming," he said patiently. "I warned you. Now stay still."

He hefted his pickax, aimed towards the box, then paused. One foot rested on the metal box. One hand still gripped the bloodied rag he'd left on the workbench.

"Artemis Blythe was on that call," he said, glancing back at the row of monitors over his bench. "Strange, isn't it?"

Sobs now. Still muffled.

How tedious.

"Do you mind?" he asked. "I'm trying to make a point here."

More insistent tapping. It was difficult to strike the metal frame with her hands bound. But *that* had been her fault. He'd asked her not to struggle. Not to fight back. He sighed, shaking his head, taking a couple of practice swings with his pick-axe. He still had it, too.

At his age... he nodded in appreciation as the axe swung through the air with a *swish.*

"Of all the people I expected to find Sierra," he said slowly, "I was surprised to see *her.* Do you know Artemis?"

He waited, listening.

No response now. She'd gone quiet. Still. Shit. He was too tired to go out and find another. So with a faint huff he said, "Move your head back, all right? Hear me?" And then he swung.

The pick gouged into the metal, puncturing. He swung again. And again. He waited a few moments, studying the new perforation in the side of the metal storage container. He glanced at the padlock, making sure it was secure.

Then he paused, listening.

Breathing. Faint, desperate, gulping breaths. He grinned, patting a hand against the metal box. "Marvelous! I was worried you might have collapsed. Don't worry—Sierra lasted nearly two days. I'm sure you can make it too, hmm?" He patted his hand against the top of the metal box, humming to himself as he did. He leaned his pick back against the side of the metal compartment, considering what he'd seen on the camera feed.

Even as he thought it, he watched as fuzz erupted across the screen.

They'd found the camera.

More accurately, *she* had found the camera.

He'd often wondered if he ought to introduce himself to Artemis. He'd studied her with some interest over the last twenty years. He'd known about Ms. Blythe long before the news.

Of course, that was because he'd been the one to introduce the Ghost-killer to these games...

Everyone needed a mentor. And he was the best there was.

That was why they called him the Professor, after all. He'd shown the Ghost-killer everything he'd known. He'd studied the Blythe family first of course.

He tapped a finger against his chin. Now, Otto was in priso n... Tommy was in the mob... Helen was... well, a tragedy that.

But the one Blythe whose story was still being written?

Little Artemis.

That was what Otto used to call his daughter. Little Artemis. He smiled at the memories. Smiled fondly, thinking of the time he'd spent sitting across that table, in that diner, during the rain storm. Face to face they'd spoken. The first time they'd ever met.

Not all mentor-student relationships ended *well* of course.

He'd been the one to make the call.

The Ghost-killer had grown dangerous. Prideful. In no small part due to *little Artemis.*

The Professor could remember the conversation well. *She's got what it takes. Give her a few years.*

One of the strangest conversations. It was then he'd made the decision to have the Ghost-killer arrested. A hard choice, a tough decision. Sentimentality had prevented him from choosing to simply handle the issue through his normal meth-ods.

His fingers trailed against the haft of his pick.

Ultimately, though, it had all ended rather poorly. He regretted it. But he wondered... the Ghost-killer had been adamant. *She has what it takes. Give her a few years.*

Perhaps now was the perfect chance.

He'd intended to play a game with the police. He'd known after the burning they would find his grove. He'd known questions would arise.

The game, though...

A distraction. A smoke screen.

He'd still let them play it, but in doing so, they would miss what was right under their noses. And he would have a first-hand chance to see if *little Artemis* really was as impressive a specimen as he'd been told.

He truly, *truly* hated when he only found pyrite instead of ore.

Empty playthings... posers... faux.

It was these pretenders that he buried deep.

They deserved it after all.

He patted the metal once more, then called out, "Hang on there—we're going for a little trip. Try not to scream too loudly, or I'll have to come in there. Neither of us will like that..." he paused, considering this. Then amended, "Well... *you* won't."

And he grabbed the handle and began dragging it, causing it to scrape across the dusty workshop floor, towards the door. He could already hear his truck idling outside.

CHAPTER 9

She sat in the back seat of the car, peering out the window at the fog circling the small lake... Not Pinelake, but rather another, even smaller community, fifteen miles east.

Grant had rented her an apartment in the tiny town of Welsford.

She listened as the two agents, sitting in the front seat, lobbed speculation back and forth. All three of them, driving towards the small apartment she'd been given, were doing their very best to figure out the Professor's clue.

Artemis' own car was being brought by the local police as a favor to Grant. Artemis simply hadn't wanted to brave the roads following a panic-laced afternoon. Sometimes, a woman simply couldn't face *everything*.

And Forester and Wade hadn't minded. They were going to get rooms in the area, anyway—and though Welsford didn't have a hotel, it did have a few houses on the lake that one could book online.

"What if the clues are fake," Wade was saying, monotone as ever. "He's probably just playing with us."

"He definitely is playing," Forester said, "But I don't know if that means they're fake. I mean, think about them. It's clearly a reference to the Wizard of Oz."

Artemis found Forester in the rearview mirror, her eyebrows up, impressed. Sitting in the car with two muscled figures for protection had been a marked improvement to the vulnerability she'd felt back in that forest. Now, she was breathing easier, thinking clearer.

"He called me *Little* Artemis. Sort of trilling the middle part."

The two figures looked back at her.

"Road!" Wade snapped.

Forester veered, peeking back just in time to avoid a merging semi. He didn't seem to care, though, and turned promptly back to look at Artemis. "What's that mean?"

"Please," she said, "watch the road."

Forester shrugged, turned back and glanced in the mirror. "Little Artemis?"

"It's something my father used to call me... A family nickname." She shivered at the recollection, wrinkling her nose. "But I can't think of any articles that used it. I don't know *how* he would've known unless he was in contact with my father."

Or somehow involved in Helen's disappearance... Artemis shivered and said quickly, "Have we identified any of the bodies yet?"

"Still working on it," Forester shot back. "As you can imagine, we're having to call a couple different offices to help out."

Artemis sighed but nodded. She leaned back in the chair, plucking at her seat belt like a guitar string. She studied the back of Forester's head.

"The first toy was empty of a heart," she murmured. She frowned, still troubled by the thought that this killer was in contact with her father. Was she just being paranoid? There had been times in the past when she'd assumed some connection that didn't exist.

"Heart, right," Forester said. "That was the tin man."

"Mhmm... And empty of a brain," Artemis said.

"Scarecrow," Wade supplied. Forester flashed his partner a sarcastic thumbs up which got slapped down over the gearshift.

"Empty of a soul, though..." Artemis said slowly, frowning. "The lion lacked courage. Is that what it means?"

"Been a while since I've seen the Wizard of Oz," said Forester with a shrug. "Besides, you're the puzzle solver. I just lift heavy things. Wade keeps me around for my good looks."

Desmond grunted. He glanced in the mirror, watching Artemis, waiting.

She wasn't sure she particularly liked this role. She considered her options, pressing her lips tightly together. The last time she'd tried to crack a riddle had been the postcards. The mistake had been focusing on the letters and sentences themselves. Rather than the material.

Her father had used the cards to smuggle drugs *not* information.

The first toy was empty of her heart. The second toy was empty of a brain. And the third toy was empty of a soul.

Three women he'd trapped... Nearby? Artemis shivered, trying not to imagine what Sierra had gone through. According to Forester, the woman was still recovering at the hospital; they'd speak with her in the morning once she regained consciousness.

"Heart. Brain... soul..." she murmured beneath her breath, frowning. "A soul has religious connotations. Is there a connection there?"

"The Wizard of Oz," said Forester. "A wizard... a soul?"

Wade glanced at the tall man. "What exactly do you think religion is..."

"You're telling me they don't believe in souls?"

"They don't believe in *wizards*."

Forester snorted. "Nice try."

Artemis said, "He was playing games when I first called him. Answering instantly, acting like he knew where I was. He wanted to spook me. Wanted to make an impression... Wanted to..." She frowned, considering this. The problem with narcissists was they always had to be the smartest person in the room. So they stacked the deck.

The postcards hadn't *had* any riddle. The issue had been the paper. The framing of the cards.

"We have to look at the framing," she said suddenly, perking up.

Forester glanced back again and this time Wade grabbed for the steering wheel to keep them in a straight line.

"What does that mean?" Forester said, wrestling control back and keeping five miles below the speed limit as he so often did, as if he couldn't be bothered to go anything other than his own pace.

"It means... I'm wrong about what he said."

"How so?"

"I cut off the frame. The start and end. What he *actually* said," she continued, murmuring, playing the conversation in her mind. "Was this: *well, as you wish.* The first toy was empty of her heart. The second toy was empty of a brain. And the third toy was empty of a soul. Good luck."

"And?"

"I think..." Artemis hesitated, shaking her head. "There's no way for me to know for sure, but I wonder if the parts about the empty heart or brain are simply descriptors of how he perceives his victims. But *well, as you wish.* And also, *Good luck.* Are the real clues." Artemis considered this for a moment then nodded once. "It's worth keeping in mind. Nothing concrete, of course."

Forester suddenly drummed his fingers against the glove compartment. "Wishing well," he said. "Think about it. Well, as you wish. Good luck. It has the words in it. A wishing well. You use it for good luck."

Artemis nodded slowly. She'd noticed the words as well but hadn't wanted to jump to any rash conclusions. "We don't *know* if that's—"

"Not important if we *know.* Just important we keep moving."

Artemis hesitated. In a way, she agreed with Forester. She closed her eyes, considering their options. It wasn't much to go on. She shook her head. "Do we know anything about that mineshaft?" she said.

Forester shot a look at Wade, who quickly pulled his phone from his pocket, already opening the search browser.

Artemis similarly withdrew her device. It was strange not to even have an identification of the victims or their survivor.

She could feel herself growing impatient at the thought of waiting for the coroner's report.

She began typing in her search bar, looking for information about the mineshaft they'd found. Before she'd gotten too far, though, Agent Wade suddenly clicked his tongue. "Got something." Before anyone could prompt him, he went on. "Looks like that area had a history of gold rush rumors back in the mid eighteen hundreds."

"Rumors?" Artemis said.

"Mhmm. No actual evidence gold was taken from that mountain. But that didn't stop people from mining in secret."

"What do you mean secret? Umm—oh, wait, never mind—I think I found the article you're looking at."

Wade shot her a look as Artemis quickly scanned the information on her browser. It was an old blog post from an amateur prospector attempting to advertise his self-published panhandling almanac as well as an upcoming *tell-all* book about the sordid secrets of the family that owned the land. The blogger, according to the About section, had dug on the property for a couple of years before looking into the veracity himself. And that's when, according to the website, he'd discovered the sham. The information presented had citations in certain newspaper compilations dating back to the 1850s. Artemis studied the blog, taking snapshots in her mind of the relevant text.

As she did, she spotted a small text bubble pop up next to her thumb.

You in the area yet?

Jamie Kramer.

She felt her heart quicken briefly and couldn't quite say why. Or, at least, she *could* but didn't want to especially not to herself. Things with Jamie were... so strange.

She shook her head, swiping the bubble out of the way, then murmuring, "Prospectors would come from all around," she murmured. "They would trespass on the land and start building their own tunnels, certain they'd find gold in the mountains. A lot of tall tales had spread... Hmm," she hesitated. "Looks like the owner of the land in eighteen-thirty-six was a man named Eleazar Watkins. Mr. Watkins attempted to sell the mountain at a premium... Possibly he was the source of those rumors about gold, hoping to boost the price."

"Secret gold miners?" Forester said, frowning and wrinkling his nose. "What's it with this area and gold?" he asked. "Didn't that other case also involve—"

"Yes," Artemis murmured. "But that's the distinction. There is *no gold.* It's only make-believe. Prospectors found nothing. For a hundred and fifty years. Nothing."

"Empty," Wade said simply.

Artemis and Forester both went quiet, staring at Wade.

"Empty," Forester said slowly. "You're right. The mountains are empty. The mine shafts were empty. No gold. Not for—what did you say? Hundred years?"

"Hundred and fifty," Artemis said.

"Well, shit," Forester muttered. "Think our killer is somehow appraised of the history? What connection does he have to it, do you think?"

"No clue," Artemis said, sighing slowly. She paused briefly, realizing she wasn't nearly as hesitant as she once had been to voice her opinions around the FBI agents. She hoped this meant she was growing more confident. She had agreed to consult for one reason, though. And she couldn't forget it.

Confirmed identities would come in the next few days, she hoped. Even the thought of discovering that Helen had been buried in that mineshaft, or beneath those trees, felt as if it would crush her.

But also... *Little Artemis.* Did all these murderers in the Pacific Northwest somehow have connections to her father? To her past?

Or was she being paranoid?

She'd once read that twenty percent of all known serial killers came from a two-hundred-mile radius around Seattle. From this area. From her hometown.

Was it something in the water?

Something in the gloomy weather?

Or just something passed down, generation to generation, like a morbid, sickly craft.

She sighed. There were questions layered on questions. She didn't know which ones to focus on. Whatever the case... if the killer was telling the truth—if he'd really murdered more than sixty people over decades... Then he was a man who knew how to conceal himself. How to hide his tracks.

This was the part that troubled her most.

Why was he coming out of the woodwork *now?* Why was he playing games with them... *now.*

Why hide his sordid little secret for twenty-five years? But then all of a sudden, now, start playing games with law enforcement?

Something was off. Something very wrong.

But the only way to find out what was to keep digging. Deeper and deeper.

She returned her attention to her phone. A second little bubble of text. This time from Cynthia Washington.

Here's the new opening Radesh has been using...

Artemis didn't click this link either. Her good friend and chess analyst had been helping Artemis prepare for the up-coming blitz tournament. Cynthia and her husband, Henry, had endured tragedy of their own recently. Artemis had actually flown to Chicago to help them find out the truth behind their grandson's death.

Something about that experience had only brought Artemis and the Washingtons even closer together. She now had an even stronger fondness for her two analysts. When she thought of them, she couldn't help but feel happy, imagining how many years the two of them had been together, best friends through thick and thin.

It also left her with a pang of grief.

At thirty-years-old, as pathetic as it was, she'd only ever dated one person. And not even that... What she and her childhood sweetheart had experienced in the mountains behind the Kramer residence hadn't been dating so much as mild flirting under the moonlight. If she was honest, Artemis had *never* dated anyone. Never had a real relationship whatsoever. She had only kissed one boy—and she'd just ignored his text.

The Washingtons had something that aroused a grief and a joy in her. She wasn't sure how both emotions could co-exist. A flare of emotion sent her fingers moving. She typed rapidly, answering Jamie first.

Yeah! Am back. Wanna meet up?

She hesitated. Deleted this last sentence. Tried again.

Yeah! Am back. How are you?

She deleted the last sentence again, cursing herself briefly and pressing her cheek against the cold glass of the vehicle as they continued to coast towards the small town Grant had set her up in.

Then, thinking of the Washingtons again, and goaded by little more than petty envy, she texted.

Yeah! Am back. Let's meet up!

She pressed send before she could second guess herself. It was like playing an opening move without considering the ramifications. The sort of thing every analyst and coach she'd ever had would have lambasted her for.

But sometimes...

She just shook her head.

Life wasn't chess. As much as she sometimes wished it was.

That message sent, she turned her attention to Cynthia's. She didn't have time to watch the video link of the full analysis of the world champion's newest tactic, but she simply typed back. *Thanks much! Appreciated! How's Henry doing?*

She sent and moved back to the article, listening as Wade and Forester were engaged in conversation.

"The Wishing Well," Wade was saying, nodding as he did. "It's right there."

Artemis suddenly perked up. "What did you say?" Her text messages were momentarily forgotten.

Wade looked back at her. He wiggled his phone. "The property's name," he said. "What it was called back in the eighteen-fifties. It was known as the Wishing Well track. And the ranch built on it... Huh. Good Luck and trouble."

"Good luck... and trouble," Forester said. "Holy shit. That means... the women—the ones he's taken—they're on the same property. That's what it means, right?" His voice was rising in volume and excitement. Artemis considered this but didn't disagree. It made some amount of sense, and she had to agree with Forester's comment from earlier.

Moves in this sordid game couldn't always be calculated, thought about for hours and only then executed. Lives were on the line. Which meant women would die if they didn't take *some* shot in the dark.

And it was the dark that they turned back towards.

Forester spun the wheel, cutting across two lanes of traffic, hopping a median, slicing across double yellow lines and then speeding back towards the mountain.

Horns blared as Forester veered in front of an extermination van.

Wade was already placing a call. "Search and rescue teams," he was saying into his phone, his words steady and regimented like soldiers marching in step off to battle. "Yes—same location. Now. Yes, right now—night search. Get a couple of lights in the sky. Helis. Good thinking. Out."

They raced right back in the direction they'd come from.

The Wishing Well property with *The Good Luck and Trouble* ranch. Had she been right about the killer's clue? The framing itself being the point? Or had she just consigned three women to their deaths? And what was the killer's connection to all of this anyway?

The questions only grew murkier in her mind as the skies themselves bled ink.

Darkness swept the horizon, and with it came an eerie gloom.

CHAPTER 10

Three hours they'd combed the woods, and now Artemis was exhausted, eyes heavy, fingers buzzing. She watched from the old, gravel road, peering up at the mountain where flashlights crisscrossed through the dark. Search teams, five-strong, moved along the slopes, tracking the *Wishing Well* property line which spanned some thousand acres.

Helicopters buzzed overhead, spotlights beaming down to aid the searchers or pick out anything untoward.

And while Artemis had broken a sweat, a fingernail and nearly her ankle while moving through the dark woods at night, it had been her idea to check the ranch itself.

Now, she moved up the asphalt road, with Forester and Wade leading the way like a couple of attack dogs.

The two men were also drenched in sweat, glaring deeply, footsteps thumping against the road as they moved towards the old, abandoned structure.

The Good Luck and Trouble ranch house was little more than three weathered walls. One wall had been smashed. The roof was gone. An old barn behind the ranch was leaning so far over she thought a gust of wind might topple it.

Eleazar Watkins, one hundred and fifty years ago, had attempted to sell this very land, using empty promises of gold in empty tunnels built in secret on the side of his mountain.

But now, far more sordid things were being discovered buried in the land.

"Who's the current owner?" Forester asked as he marched ahead of them, his long legs covering the distance twice as fast.

Artemis shot a look at Wade who had the information on his phone, but he lobbed the look back at her, likely deciding she'd already memorized the information.

Which she had.

She hesitated, coughed delicately then said, "According to the deed Wade screenshotted, it's the Watkins estate. None of them currently live in the area, but they have a caretaker on site. Supposedly he lives near the ranch house—I can't see how."

She frowned at the worn structure again. Pockets of mold were visible even from here as one of the helicopters chattered overhead, its light flashing past the building.

"Caretaker got a name?" Forester said.

Artemis nodded. "Jeb Arthur."

"Wait what?" Forester paused now, turning sharply back to look at her.

Artemis winced. "Umm... Jeb Arthur? It was listed on the bill of sale. Why?"

"Because," Forester snapped, then his fingers followed suit, clicking towards Wade.

"Use your words, Cam," Wade said.

"Give me your damn phone, Desmond."

Artemis glanced between them, trying to place what exactly had shifted in the mood. Both men were frowning now as Wade raised his phone and turned on the screen. When Forester tried to snatch it though, Wade—the broader man—slapped the taller man's fingers away. He read something on his screen.

"What?" Artemis asked.

"Earlier, up that slope," Forester said, nodding his head towards where they'd left the northern search party to check out the ranch, "Wade got an email on that number Sierra has tattooed."

"So?"

"So," Forester said, "That number was once listed to a Jebediah Arthur. He dropped the number two years ago, switching over. But now..."

It was Artemis' turn to stare at Wade. He still held his phone up, illuminating his features while nodding quickly, confirming Forester's words.

Artemis hesitated, a prickle now spreading down her spine. "I thought you said the number was a burner phone."

"It was," Forester shot back. "But the number itself might have been transferred. What are the odds that our ranch caretaker so happened to—two years ago—use the very phone number our creep called us on?"

"Does this guy have a record?" Artemis asked.

Wade was already shaking his head. "Just checked," he said. "Nothing showing up. Unless the name is fake. Can't find much about the guy."

"Well," Artemis said, "He's supposed to be living on the property."

All three of them glanced back towards the run-down building. Now, Forester still in the lead, they reached the base of the old, worn ranch house.

Forester took a couple of steps up the moldered stairs but then cursed as his foot slammed through a soggy section, puncturing the wood more than splintering it.

"Dammit," Forester muttered, ripping his foot out.

Artemis shook her head. "You keep doing that," she murmured. "Falling into things."

"Call it a knack, Checkers. Doesn't look like anyone's home. Heck, place doesn't *look* like a home."

The closer they'd gotten to the creepy, derelict structure, the more frightened Artemis had become and the more animated and excited Forester seemed.

Agent Wade didn't care either way; he walked brusquely, keeping up with Forester but keeping his expression impassive.

Forester leaned forward to peer at the rest of the structure. As he did, though, he clicked his tongue and shook his head. "Nothing. Charred wood. The place is junk." He looked back at her and raised an eyebrow. "You're sure this caretaker lives on the property?"

"None of the search parties found anything," Wade said quietly.

Artemis nodded. She knew that he meant the search parties hadn't found any structures or homes on the property. But they also hadn't found any sign of the supposed women. It bothered her that they were taking the killer's say so as their evidence.

It was distinctly possible that the killer had been lying to them about everything. That he was playing with them.

Agent Grant had made a good point earlier. They didn't even know if they had the right killer. Or, if there weren't multiple killers. This thought had occurred to Artemis while moving around in the dark, avoiding branches and brambles, and wishing desperately she had reconsidered her choice of coming back to Washington.

There were too many unanswered questions.

"When Mr. Arthur did have a phone number registered, did he have to provide an address?"

Wade was still studying his phone. It took a second, but then he said, "Same as that bill of sale you mentioned. He supposedly lives here."

They all looked doubtfully back at the three moldered walls.

But then, Forester frowned; he said, quietly, "Tracks. Big old truck." He was waving a finger towards the barn.

Artemis and Wade followed as Forester hopped down from the step he'd broken and began to move quickly towards the large, tilting barn.

The two helicopters crisscrossing the mountain were now moving around the other side, helping one of the southern search parties.

No radio chatter, suggesting that, still, no one had found anything.

But Forester was picking up his pace now, dragging his foot along the path, scraping dirt, but also indicating where a large tread had left marks in the dust. As far as Artemis knew, there had been no trucks in the 1850s.

Wade and Artemis had to quicken to keep up, but Forester was now pointing, and his other hand had moved to his hip, hovering near his weapon.

He didn't speak but kept a finger indicating.

And then Artemis spotted it. A small camera, pointing toward the road.

Forester stepped off the path, moving in a faint circle, through tall weeds, careful to keep out of the line of sight of the camera attached to the large barn.

Artemis followed.

And then she spotted something. A flicker of light from the leaning barn.

Her mind was spinning.

Good luck. One of his clues. The name of the ranch house.

And suddenly, she was frowning, glancing back towards that old structure.

Almost despite herself, attracted by her own curiosity, she moved away from the two men, hastening back towards the burnt-out husk of the house. Forester and Wade, distracted by the barn, didn't notice her peel off but instead continued their quick stride towards the tilting structure.

Artemis reached the open ranch house.

Why would he use the name of the ranch house unless...

She stared at the moldered walls, her eyes moving down towards the floor. Much of it had been torn up. Mounds of dirt had replaced sections of wooden flooring. But there, in the back, nestled between two walls, at a ninety-degree angle, she spotted a wooden frame and beneath it, three stone steps leading into the dark.

She stared at the steps now, hesitant, still standing outside the wall, peering in.

"Guys," she murmured, calling over her shoulder.

Forester and Wade were moving beneath the camera now, having avoided its line of sight, both approaching a small side door in the barn, each of them with their firearms drawn.

"Guys?" Artemis said still softly.

But Forester was now stepping back, preparing to kick down the wooden door. The chatter of helicopter blades momentarily distracted Artemis.

She frowned then turned back towards the stone steps. "H-hello?" she whispered.

She knew she needed to wait for the FBI agents to rejoin her before attempting to investigate those stairs and the apparent basement on her own.

She would wait, she decided. It wasn't like she would be much use in breaking down a barn door, anyway.

She idled by the remnants of the torn wall, watching as Forester swung his long leg. *Crack!* The old door shattered. For a moment, Artemis thought the barn itself might collapse.

But then, structure still standing, Wade slammed his linebacker shoulder into the already broken door, and the two men disappeared into the dark barn, moving under the security camera.

The camera, though, Artemis realized, was *on* the barn, but directly facing the house.

In fact...

It was angled towards those stone stairs under the wooden frame.

Artemis exhaled slowly, trying to calm herself. There was no risk in waiting. No gunshots either resounding into the night. That was good, at least.

As she stood, watching the barn, listening for sounds of violence...

She heard something else.

Perhaps in response to her own murmuring from earlier.

But she heard it distinctly.

A faint, desperate shout. Muffled, though. Scarcely even there. More like a whimper on the wind, plucked like some bauble by a zephyr and presented to Artemis' ears.

Part of her, certainly, wanted to ignore it.

But she heard it again. A louder, more desperate exclamation.

Coming from the dark.

Coming up those stone steps in the run-down ranch house, the sound echoing out of the apparent basement.

Help...

That's what it sounded like. A desperate, pleading... *Help!*

Artemis shivered. She was just hearing things, certainly. No reason to get ahead of herself. "Guys?" She called out, louder now.

No gunshots, still. No sign or sound of a struggle. But Forester and Wade were still absent. She didn't want to call too loudly in case they were slowly maneuvering through the barn. If someone was lurking in the dark, she didn't want to alert them to the presence of the FBI.

But again, she heard the faint whisper of a sound.

A desperate, pleading hum of minimal noise.

She knew she'd heard it. No rationalizing herself out of it. There it was. *Help!*

She shot a look back towards the barn. "Come on," she murmured. "Come *on!*" She willed the agents to emerge, to declare the all-clear. But it didn't happen.

Now, she was worried about Forester and Wade.

She was also worried about herself.

But she was doubly concerned for the source of that noise.

Good luck.

The first toy was empty of her heart.

Artemis considered this a moment longer, then cursed and stepped over the charred husk of the remaining evidence of a once-existent wall.

Nothing happened.

Not that she'd expected it would.

She tentatively stepped through the dust, over worn floorboards, towards the stone stairs. The desperate sounds had faded now, but this only served to propel her forward even faster.

What if something had happened?

The first toy was empty of her heart.

Just a descriptor?

No... No, it couldn't be. Not with a man like this. He was playing with them. He wanted them to know he was smarter, he was clever.

Empty of her heart... What did it mean? Some type of warning? A threat?

She hurried forward, rushing towards the stone stairs now. Trying to avoid tripping over the wooden floorboards. She reached the stairs, one hand bracing against the wooden frame.

This frame was not worn like the rest of the ranch house. The wood was sturdy beneath her fingers, though, someone had gone to great trouble to stain it with ash in an attempt to hide it.

She hovered at the top step, trying not to think too poorly of herself. Her hesitation was caution wasn't it? Not cowardice.

Her stomach was twisting, a knot forming in her belly.

Artemis closed her eyes briefly, and then, with a puff of air, she took the plunge, stepping into the dark, taking one stair at a time, and descending into the black.

There was still no sound behind her. No sign of the agents.

She was very much alone, moving into the unknown. The only company she had was the faint prickle of dread tiptoeing along her arms and down her spine.

CHAPTER 11

She took the bottom step into the basement and was forced to use the light app on her smartphone in order to see in the dark.

Artemis glanced around the dark space, moving the light on her phone as she did. She stepped over what looked like a tangle of rusted springs, redirecting her light in order to navigate the dark space. She exhaled slowly, holding her breath and her tongue as her eyes adjusted to the bright beam from her phone light.

"H-hello?" she murmured, glancing around the empty space. She took a cautious step off the bottom stair, then went suddenly still, staring towards the item in the middle of the room.

A metal box.

She spotted holes punctured in one side. The metal box was about the size of a sideways refrigerator. She exhaled slowly, feeling a prickle along her face as goosebumps crawled along her skin.

She took a tentative step towards the box.

"H-hello?" she tried again.

Another, muffled response. Definitely coming from the metal container.

Artemis threw caution to the wind, then. Taking three sprinting strides towards the box, her pulse pounding in horror. "Hang on!" she yelled. "I'm coming. It's going to be... fine..." she trailed off, going suddenly still, fingers hovering over the metal handle. She spotted the padlock but also spotted something else.

A lifetime of training for the smallest details. She wasn't sure if it was the way the light had swung one way then the other or perhaps sheer luck.

Or maybe the niggling in the back of her mind. *Empty... heart...*

But as she reached for the handle, she stiffened. And then she spotted the two needles embedded in the grip. Needles pointing inwards, nearly invisible. They looked coated with some sort of sap-like substance.

She swallowed, then, casting desperately about, she searched for any item she might use to shatter the padlock. A brick by an old storage space caught her eye. She hastened over, snatched it up and returned, hefting it in one hand.

She aimed for the storage container, exhaled, then brought it swinging down.

It took her a couple of tries, but she managed to smash the flimsy, rusted lock. She turned her attention then towards the needles she'd spotted, swinging the brick again.

The needles broke off. This done, she wrapped her sleeve around her hand and, carefully, avoiding the section where the needles had been, she flung open the container.

A woman, hands bound, was staring up at Artemis, breathing heavily, her eyes widened in terror. By the looks of things, a duct tape gag had been torn off—some tape still adhered to her cheek and beneath her lower lip.

The woman had tears streaming down her face.

This was good, as far as Artemis could tell. The woman wasn't so dehydrated she couldn't cry.

"I'm with the FBI!" Artemis blurted. "I'm with the FBI! It's going to be okay. I promise you."

The woman's eyes brimmed with tears again, and she stared at Artemis, trembling and shaking her head. Artemis reached in, gently guiding the woman into a sitting position while quickly scanning her arms, abdomen, legs, searching for any injuries.

The tears continued as the woman shakily allowed herself to be helped out of the box.

The tears, in a way, were another reminder of something Artemis didn't have. She hadn't cried in nearly fifteen years. The last time she remembered weeping was when her father had been led away.

Since then...

Nothing. As if a part of her had died that day.

Still, that didn't mean she couldn't feel compassion. And now, with one arm, she helped the woman steadily to her feet, guiding her away from that awful container. "You should sit down," Artemis murmured. "Are you dizzy?"

But the woman was shaking her head, stumbling forward now. She stammered, "I—I thought you were..." A big swallow of air. "Him." She shot a panicked look into the darker corners but then shook her head, moving back up the stairs.

Artemis helped guide her, allowing the woman to lean stiffly on her arm. She detected the scent of perfume, though, it had mingled with body odor. She also felt the woman's frail arm trembling in her grasp. She helped the woman up the stairs, out of the horrible basement and led her out of the abandoned house, through the three walls and towards the barn.

"Forester!" Artemis called now. They'd had long enough, she decided, to clear the barn. "Wade!"

But neither man emerged to help her. Artemis frowned, still serving as something of a crutch for the poor woman.

"P-please. Don't... don't let him find me again," the woman was saying, sobbing. "Please, don't..."

"Never," Artemis said firmly. She glanced towards the barn again. "Forester! Wade! We need paramedics! Now!"

She thought she spotted movement inside the barn, but no one emerged. Artemis shook her head in frustration. "Here," she said gently, "let me help you sit here—is that okay? The moss is very soft. It will be comfortable."

The woman hesitated but then reluctantly allowed Artemis to lower her to the ground. She tucked her legs up under her frail form, still trembling, wrapping her arms around her legs.

Artemis then flashed a quick, comforting smile. She was already dialing 9-1-1 as she turned, beginning to hasten towards the barn. "I'll be right back!" she called.

The woman started shaking again, sobbing. "N-no! P-p-please!" she said.

Artemis glanced back. She could see tears still tracing through the woman's muddy face. The woman's hair was tangled, unwashed, and her clothing looked similarly dirt-streaked. Artemis wondered how long the woman had been in the killer's grasp.

She stared at the figure leaning against the fence post on a patch of moss. The woman stared at the ground, her face cast in shadow now as if she were deeply ashamed. The tears continued to tumble. "P-please don't leave me in the dark," The woman said in a very small voice.

Artemis swallowed, staring. Then she nodded quickly. "Of course not. Here, take my phone. Shine the light this way. You're on the line with 9-1-1. Call an ambulance; do you know where we are? No? Tell them we're at the Good Luck and Trouble ranch on the Wishing Well property. Can you do that?" Artemis gently handed the phone towards the woman. As the light flashed across the figure's form, she winced, holding a hand up to block the glare.

Artemis wondered how long the woman had been trapped in that horrible box. "I'll be right back," Artemis insisted. "I just have to check on two agents—in that barn. I'll be quick. Okay? I promise I won't leave you."

The woman reached out, grabbing at Artemis' arm, holding on tight. "P-please," she whispered. "Thank you. Thank you." Another sob. "He said," she murmured, "That the handle was poisoned."

Artemis stiffened. "What?"

"The handle on the-the..." she trailed off. "Some poison. It was supposed to cause a heart attack." The woman shook her head.

Artemis just stared, then scowled. *Empty heart.* A poison needle to inflict a heart attack. She glared directly at the camera over the barn, flashing her middle finger at the camera. Then, gently, she said, "I'll be right back. Wait, hear that? 9-1-1?" Artemis spoke louder, realizing a voice was coming over the speaker of her phone.

But now, her concern for her partners was rising. Artemis had to extricate her hand, leaving her phone in the grip of the shaking woman and then turning to sprint back towards the barn.

Artemis broke into a jog, calling over her shoulder. "Call the ambulance!" And then Artemis reached the barn.

She shot glances back towards where the woman was speaking in fumbling sentences into the phone.

Artemis reached the barn, desperate, shoving open the door.

And then she realized what had delayed the agents.

Forester and Wade were both pointing their weapons towards a man in the middle of the barn. A small mattress rested on the floor. Some straw poked out from beneath bedding. A backpack and a small, campfire teapot—blackened from use—also rested against a support beam for the tilting barn.

The man was shooting nervous looks between the two agents, swallowing as his head swiveled.

The moment Artemis showed up, though, he let out a yelp. "Hey! Hey! Watch it!" he screamed.

And Artemis realized, now, that he was also holding a gun.

A large, double-barrel shotgun which he was moving back and forth between Forester and Wade.

Artemis felt another prickle along her skin.

"Sir," Forester was saying in an even tone, "You're going to want to calm down, please. No one has to get shot."

Wade kept his gun raised. Artemis had never seen such steady hands gripping a weapon. The ex-Special Forces operative looked the picture of calm and collected as he pointed his firearm towards the man with the shotgun.

"I told you once, and I won't again," the man snarled, shaking his head. "Get out of my house! You have no right!" The fellow in question had wide, frightened eyes, a look like a transient, but was surprisingly well-groomed. A neat beard, trimmed, plucked eyebrows and clean skin. His hair was even combed back, though, a bit of straw had managed to lodge just above his ear.

The man kept his grip on his shotgun, but both hands were trembling.

"Lower the weapon," Forester advised. There wasn't even a hint of fear in his voice. "Now. I'm a pretty cool cat, Jeb, but my partner here once shot a man for sneezing funny."

Jeb glanced in alarm at Wade but then back at Forester. "How do you know my name?" he yelped.

Artemis spotted where the bedding on the ground had been disheveled and a disturbed section of hay indicating a recent tussle. She noticed Forester had strands of the hay stuck to the back of his misbuttoned suit jacket.

And while she didn't know what had transpired before her arrival, she knew if bullets started flying, no one was getting out of this unscathed.

"Lower your weapon, bud," Forester said, extending a hand flat.

Jeb Arthur swallowed desperately, shaking his head. "You tell me what this is about. You're trespassing."

"You hear those choppers?" Forester shot back.

"Yeah—they had 'em by for the fires last week."

"Mhmm. They're not here for fires this time. You wanna take a guess why they've come by?"

Mr. Arthur just shook his head, his shotgun barrel trembling now to match the motion of his hands. The ranch caretaker was breathing in an erratic, rising tempo. Artemis shot a quick look back through the barn doors in the direction where she'd left their most recent victim.

She didn't want to speak, worried she might set something off. But also, she was growing worried about the woman outside—Artemis had promised to return quickly and could only imagine the fear the woman was now experiencing, left alone in the dark.

Desperately, she tried to think of a way to de-escalate the situation.

But Forester was already lowering his gun, eyes on Arthur. "Now, look here," Forester said slowly, somehow not even blinking once. "Why don't we just talk about this like adults, hmm? No need for anyone to get shot. I noticed your tattoo there—that little clover. Wouldn't be for Lucky's, would it?"

Jeb scowled, quickly tugging at his sleeve. As he did, though, his shotgun wavered, lowering for a moment.

By lowering his own weapon briefly, Forester had put Jeb off guard. But as the caretaker adjusted his sleeve, covering a tattoo of a four-leaf clover—which Artemis didn't recognize, but Forester seemed to—Forester suddenly moved.

A burst forward, legs springing, one hand already outstretched, shoving the barrel of the shotgun further towards the ground.

A sudden blast and shot erupted into the dusty floor. Jeb yelled.

Wade was already moving, too.

But Forester had ripped the gun from the hands of the ranch caretaker, flinging it off onto the straw. Wade then came in, over Forester, hitting the man in a tackle. The two men brought down their suspect, landing in the bedding.

Jeb Arthur kicked and hollered at first, but after a few seconds of struggle, he went slowly limp, exhausting himself. Wade's handcuffs *clicked* into place. Forester held the man down, cautioning him. "Stop it—no, just stop. You're coming with us."

Artemis winced, glancing at the scene. But now, guns stowed, she felt permitted to raise her voice. "I found a survivor!" she said.

The two FBI agents glanced sharply over, eyes wide. Artemis winced but nodded quickly. She jammed a finger over her shoulder. "I left her calling paramedics." And then, content that both the agents were safe and could take care of themselves, she turned and hastened back through the barn door.

As she jogged back up the dusty road, she spotted the beam of light from her phone.

She stared at it, though, and went still.

It felt as if someone had sucker punched her as the air deflated from her lungs. She spun around, looking down the fence line, then glanced back up towards the direction of the house.

"Hello?" she called out. "Ma'am?"

But the woman was nowhere to be seen.

Artemis turned one way, then the other, rushing back and picking up her phone. The light app had been left on. She held her phone, swiveling it to scan the side of the ranch house.

But no sign of the woman.

The survivor was gone.

Had she run off?

Artemis felt a prickle down her spine.

Or had something worse happened?

She shot a panicked look back towards the barn as Forester and Wade pushed Jeb Arthur in front of them. The man was glaring at the ground, but briefly, as he glanced up, his eyes met Artemis'.

Was that a note of recognition?

No... No, she was being paranoid.

She called out, louder, "Hello! Where are you?"

But no response came. Except from Forester. "So where is she?" he called out, pushing Arthur into Wade's waiting hands.

Forester broke into a jog, hastening towards her and joining her on the empty patch of old road.

But Artemis just shook her head, numb. "I... I don't know," she murmured. "She was right here. *Right* here! I found her in the basement over there. There's another metal locker with breathing holes... I don't know where she went!"

"All right, calm down, Ms. Blythe. Wade, take Arthur to the car!" Forester then pulled the radio from his belt and began issuing instructions to the search teams. "We're looking for a woman now, too. Especially keep an eye out if you see someone with her." Forester paused, finger still on the radio; he shot a quick look at Artemis. "Description?"

"Umm... Thin? Dirty." Artemis winced, wishing she'd taken the time to find out more about the woman. She hadn't even gotten a name in all the excitement. "I... I didn't really see much. It was dark down there. And out here. She looked scared..."

Forester relayed the scant information and lowered the radio. Wade was guiding the man in cuffs behind them. Artemis felt a weight of guilt settling in her gut. What had she just done? Why hadn't she just stayed with the woman?

She shook her head, scanning the old building again.

But the woman had disappeared like a ghost.

Or... far more horrifying... someone had come along and taken her.

Did Jeb Arthur have an accomplice? *Was* Mr. Arthur the accomplice? Did he have anything to do with it?

She could feel the overwhelming weight of questions, of loose ends, of terror and guilt, all coming in. A crushing burden.

She shook her head, inhaling shakily and trying to focus.

The whir of helicopter blades above rattled by, but wherever the light shone from the heli, the illumination found only empty fields.

The woman was gone.

And Artemis had let it happen.

CHAPTER 12

The guilt was secondary to the exhaustion now. It was late by the time they found themselves back at the local precinct, borrowing one of the interrogation rooms. Artemis' hand fluttered over her mouth, stifling a yawn. Even so, as she stood in the back of the interrogation room, her stomach tightened.

Another bout of guilt.

In her mind, she tried to picture the woman. The image of the way the panicked figure had hunched over Artemis' phone, like a moth seeking *some* form of light, was now burned in Artemis' brain.

What had happened to her?

She must have run off... That was it, wasn't it?

"Anything?" Artemis said suddenly, looking up as Forester joined her. Behind the tall man, down the hall, Artemis spotted where a couple of police officers were helping Wade to wrangle Jeb Arthur down the corridor.

The man was not coming quietly.

Shouts and threats and grunts of exertion—punctuating bids for freedom—accompanied the approaching suspect.

Forester, who'd already taken his turn escorting the prisoner, wiped a hand across a sweaty forehead. "Whew," he muttered, jamming his foot against the door to keep it open for their new guest. Wade was suddenly knocked into the wall as Mr. Arthur flung himself backwards, pinning the FBI agent.

The two aiding officers yelled, grabbing at Jeb and pulling him away, while Wade shoved the suspect off him.

Forester didn't react. In a way, he almost looked bored as he surveyed the approaching scene; but then he turned, shooting a quick look at Artemis.

"Nothing found yet," he said quietly, shaking his head. He tapped the radio on his holster. "They'll let us know the moment they find her."

"What if they don't find her!" Artemis exclaimed. "She was so scared, Cameron! So scared."

Another outburst down the hall prompted Forester to snort, remove his foot from the door jam and allow the interrogation room door to slowly close shut. He glanced at her now, quirking an eyebrow. "Are you all right?" he said slowly.

"N-no," she snapped back, but then realizing her tone, she swallowed and tried again. "No... I'm not. I shouldn't have left her on the road."

"You thought Wade and I were in danger. You came to help us. Can't fault that."

"But... but what if..." Artemis trailed off, trying to think. Jeb Arthur was involved somehow. That much felt certain, didn't it? His phone number had been tattooed on Sierra's arm. The killer had used that phone number. He'd been sleeping in a barn next to a burnt-out house with a kidnapped woman trapped in the basement.

Jeb Arthur was involved.

But then what had happened to the woman from the basement?

Artemis couldn't help but fear something horrible.

"I saw that basement too," Forester said, shaking his head. "I get it. Really. But if she bolted, that's on her. Not you."

"How can you say that?"

"Because," Forester said firmly, "you're going to have to learn fast on this job that you might be able to save *some* from murderers and bad guys. But you can't save *anyone* from themselves. That's their choice. She didn't trust you, or us, and ran. That's it."

"Unless someone came by and took her. Someone watching on that camera over the barn."

"That camera fed right to Mr. Arthur's own laptop hub. He was in there with us the whole time. She ran. Trust me."

Before he could go much further, though, there was a sudden burst of static over the radio. Artemis' heart skipped, and she stared wide-eyed, frozen on the tiles in the interrogation room. She gave a little flutter of her hand as if commanding Forester to answer.

Which he did.

"Agent Forester," he said quickly. "What's up?"

Another crackle, then a reply. "We found someone," the voice said. "A woman. Early-twenties. Dirt-streaked. She was locked inside an old shed we missed on the first pass." The voice sounded somewhat disgusted.

"Another woman?"

"Yeah. She was trapped, though. Bunch of stones fell on the breacher. She's being taken to the hospital now."

"Any other description of the woman?"

"She's unconscious. Headed to the hospital. No driver's license. She's... about five foot. Blonde..."

Artemis' heart plummeted, but instantly, she bit her lip hard against the reaction. They'd rescued a second woman. The rocks over the door, falling on someone's head... *Empty of a brain... Empty of a heart...* Only the empty soul remained.

Artemis shivered, shaking her head. But even so, the first woman was still missing.

"We're still combing the mountain," said the radio voice. "Getting late though."

Forester snapped, "I don't give a shit, man. We found two of them. There's another one out there. Keep an eye for traps. First location had hypodermic needles jammed in a handle."

A pause, a weary sigh. Then, "Roger. Out."

The static died.

And with it all of Artemis' hopes that they might have discovered the missing woman.

"Well," Forester said, glancing at her. "We found another. He's keeping them on the property."

"There's a third still out there," Artemis murmured. "Empty of a soul... whatever that means. And also..."

"We'll find her if she wants to be found, Artemis. Just be glad you rescued her. She's probably found her way back home as we speak and is sipping chicken noodle in a big old blanket." He gave a quick smile and a nod.

She knew he was trying to be comforting, but it didn't help. She'd messed up. The not *knowing* was the hardest part.

But maybe...

Maybe the not knowing could be remedied.

The door banged open to the interrogation room and loud voices followed. Jeb Arthur was finally wrangled into a metal chair facing the table, his hands *and* legs cuffed to the seat.

Like this, unable to move much, he resorted to snarling and yelling and threatening.

But after some time of this, like a toddler throwing a tantrum, eventually he simply tired himself out. As Forester and Wade settled in the chairs on the opposite side of the table and the interrogation room door closed, Artemis remained standing watching the suspect slumped in the chair, his dark hair disheveled now, his bangs hanging in his eyes.

When he looked up, still scowling, it was with scorn in his eyes.

Before Jeb could issue another series of colorful threats, though, Forester spoke.

The lanky agent had his usual laconic drawl and sniffed as he glanced off across the room, as if he really couldn't be bothered to pay too much attention to Mr. Arthur. A ploy, Artemis thought. Intent on getting even further under the ranch caretaker's skin.

"So, Jeb," Forester started. "Normally, I'd wine and dine. Maybe play a little footsie. But we've got a woman on that mountain of yours trapped somewhere. Hell, might even have a second woman who ran away. So... this is what we're going to do. Instead of all the preamble, why don't we hop to it, hmm?" He looked up, eyes bright. He even flashed a disarming smile. "Why don't you tell me where the women are... Save us all a lot of hassle."

Mr. Arthur was scowling now. His face had gone still, and the blood had crept from his cheeks, leaving them pale. He jerked at his hands a bit more, causing the cuffs to rattle, but then, at long last, he settled, emitting a puff of air.

Artemis fidgeted uncomfortably in the back of the room, arms crossed. Wade and Forester both sat upright, like sentries, examining this threat in the chair across from them.

At last, shifty-eyed, Jeb muttered, "What in the hell are you jawing about, Stretch?"

Forester blinked. Wade shot a quick look at his partner.

Forester tried again, "You really want to go this route? We know your phone number was used in a crime. Know that your name was on the bill of sale for the Wishing Well property. The same property where we discovered one big ol' heap of corpses. How many did you say it was? Fifty-five?"

But Arthur didn't correct Forester. Instead, he simply shook his head. "I don't know what the hell you're talking about."

"Two hells that. Thinking of visiting soon?"

"What?"

Wade interjected now. "Care to explain why a woman was found locked in the basement of the ranch house?"

Jeb Arthur leaned back now, scowling. "Come again?"

Wade shook his head.

Arthur hesitated. "A woman? She dead?"

"You tell us," Forester cut in.

"I've already told you, smartass, you all were trespassing. I have no damn clue about any dead dames."

"How didn't you know she was in that basement then?"

"Who was?"

"Think this is a game? This will all go easier if you cooperate, Jeb. Might even put a good word in for you with your executioner. Ask him to be gentle with that lethal injection of his."

Arthur went still now. He shook his head quickly. Artemis watched as his features morphed from defiant to hesitant. "You're serious?"

"Deadly."

"Nah, not about the threat, Stretch. Bodies on the mountain?"

Forester leaned in, staring at Mr. Arthur. "Sir, I'm going to ask you this once. Mostly as a favor. But are you high? Because I can't think of another reason for such a stupid question. Of course I'm serious. You think sixty-five corpses is a joke? Now where's the live one—you have a third. We found the first two, by the way."

Artemis noticed how he didn't mention that one of those two had disappeared.

But Mr. Arthur was shaking his head, aghast. Some of the veneer has faded, his jaw open. "I—I wasn't... I didn't do... Shit." He trailed off, frowning now and staring at the table.

"That's right, bud. We've got you dead to rights."

"You can't think I had anything to do with it!"

"See—this brings me right back to the high question. Because hell *yes* we think you had something to do with it. Was anyone else in on it? Hmm? What about the property owners. What are their names? The Watkins family?"

Arthur's eyes suddenly widened and he let out a little squeak of air. He recovered quickly enough, but the mention of his employer seemed to take it out of him. Artemis watched as his entire demeanor shifted, moving from defiance and shock to calculated damage control. Even the man's tone moved into something a bit more amenable. He leaned back, exhaling deeply as he did. "The Watkins family trusts me to take care of things. They are *not* involved. They haven't been near the property in years."

"Hmm, that right?" Forester said. "A thousand acre mountain paradise and these guys just leave it in your greasy hands?"

Arthur snapped, "This might be news to you, *cop*, but not everyone's definition of luxury is a bowl of mac and cheese and a handjob."

Forester pointed at himself, eyebrows rising in mock surprise. "H-how did you know about happy Tuesdays?"

"Forester," Wade growled.

Cameron leaned back again, eyes hooded, glaring at Arthur. "Did you put that woman in the basement, Jeb?"

"No!"

"Did you kill those folk on the mountain?"

"No!"

"Where's our third victim? Where did you lock her away, you sick twist?"

"I didn't do anything. To anyone. I came in late to check on some property line issues. There's a sale pending. The Watkins want nothing to do with the land after the government came in and burned half the mountain. Some type of free country." He snorted.

Forester tapped his fingers against the metal table. "You're saying you stopped by the barn, took a kip and had no *clue* there was a woman suffocating in the ranch house you're supposed to be taking care of?"

"Yeah. That's about right."

Forester snorted, shaking his head and leaning back. "Bullshit."

"Well, it's true. Not my job to piece things together for you."

Artemis listened to this back and forth. Flat-out denial with no attempt to make it palatable. Clearly, Jeb Arthur had other concerns on his mind than being arrested for murder.

Something about the way he'd reacted to the Watkins family name.

Artemis scowled to herself, considering the options. Suddenly, unable to contain herself, she blurted out, "How old are you?"

All three men glanced back towards her. Her gaze didn't waver from the suspect.

"You interested?" Jeb asked, raising his eyebrows.

"How old," she said more insistently.

Wade had his phone out again. "Thirty-two," Wade called back to Artemis.

The moment he said it, a thick silence fell. They were all doing the math. Some of those corpses were nearly two decades old. According to the phone call, some were as old as twenty-five years. Which would have meant Mr. Arthur was only seven years old at the time of the murders.

The timeline didn't match. But he certainly was behaving oddly. Jeb was shaking his head now, emitting a sudden yawn, which he seemed to have reserved for the moment Forester tried to speak again.

Forester scowled and started again. "You're going to be sitting in the cell tonight, bud. Hope it's comfortable. Unless you've got anything useful you want to add." But Arthur just shook his head, yawning again—though this time it sounded forced.

Artemis just watched the exchange, her eyes beginning to droop. She felt the urge to yawn as well but held it back.

116

She glanced at the ground briefly, considering their options. There were too many moving pieces. None of it made sense. They needed more information. They needed to speak with someone who'd *encountered* the killer.

Did she really think Jeb Arthur was the murderer?

He was defiant, belligerent and had been found only a hundred feet away from the woman Artemis had helped out of that metal locker.

But what if he was telling the truth? What if he hadn't known she was there? What if he hadn't known about the bodies on the mountain?

A thousand acres was a large stretch of land.

And why had he acted so scared at the Watkins family name?

Plus... he would have been seven years old at the time of the first murders... So clearly, if he was involved, he wasn't the only one.

No... It was too early to jump to any conclusions. They needed more information. And the only person who had met the killer in person was currently recovering at a hospital.

At least... the only person they could still locate.

She felt another surge of guilt but was already turning towards the door.

The interrogation was getting nowhere, and she needed to do some investigating of her own into the Watkins family. To find out if the wealthy family was somehow involved in all of this.

CHAPTER 13

Long ago, the Professor had decided that the best way to stay one step ahead of law enforcement, was to commit the crime in as short of a window as possible.

Which was why, sitting in the back of his sedan, peering through tinted windows, he watched the house of the soulless woman.

The third victim...

Except...

She hadn't been victimized yet.

He smirked, imagining the police and search parties moving all up and down that mountain, desperately searching, kicking over every rock and tree branch. He'd been right to trust Artemis Blythe's puzzle-solving abilities. The Wishing Well property and the Good Luck and Trouble ranch. She'd figure it out well enough.

But if he didn't get moving, she would see through the illusion.

Sierra had been his first messenger. She was safe at a hospital. She didn't know anything. At least... nothing obvious. He'd taken great care to keep her blindfolded and bound. Still... people in blindfolds could still pick up on the strangest pieces of evidence.

He needed to be more cautious in the future.

Three more empty husks, playthings, had been left on that mountain. One in the basement. Heartless. One in the shed. Brainless. But the third?

Not yet.

He could see her moving, though, just inside the large mansion at the end of the cul-de-sac, occupying a neat, two-acre parcel of land behind a manufactured lake. This woman was empty of a soul.

He had long discovered, despite people's best assurances, that most mine shafts were empty. Most people were pretend. Humans liked to act as if they were something else, mimicking figures they saw on television, or in their favorite movies, but really, humans were all the same.

And this woman, this soulless husk, had been a great disappointment.

He reached across the front seat, his hand resting on the handle of his pick. He could remember the early days, more than twenty years ago, the first time he had broken into someone's house.

He could remember the exhilaration, the thrill.

That was the part they never mentioned about murder.

It was just so much fun.

But it also served a purpose.

Over the course of years, he had learned to only target those who couldn't protect themselves. People no one would miss.

His most recent two victims, he had picked up hitchhiking. Other options, over the years, had included prostitutes from the town over or unsuspecting women who lived alone and wouldn't be missed for days, if not weeks.

He felt a flicker of excitement.

He had chosen to reveal himself to the police. Having been active, undetected for more than twenty years, with only a few mentions in the papers of missing women or suspicious break-ins, he was now playing games with the federals.

And the reason was simple.

A reason that most could understand.

Retirement.

Not from his favorite pastime, of course. He would be spending time with playthings until he was dead and gone. But rather, a comfortable retirement.

After what had happened with the Ghost-killer, not to mention the other murderers he shared a state with, the Professor had realized something difficult to admit.

The police were getting better at their jobs. The FBI had more technology than ever. It was hard now to do anything without some recording device or telephone capturing it on camera.

The burning of the forest, clearing the debris over his favorite mine shafts, had been the final straw. Not to mention... Carl was dying.

But yes, it was time to move to a different country. He smiled at the thought. He had always wanted to travel. But in order for that to happen, he needed the money.

A lot of money.

And the best part?

This game with the police was going to get him every penny.

It was a genius move. One that would have those federals scratching their heads for months until they figured out what had happened. And by then, he would be long gone.

There was no gold in those mountains.

But he did know where to find some.

Once this was over, everything would change. Artemis Blythe was the sign he had been looking for. She shared the blood of the Ghost-killer. She had been clever enough to find the ranch. But, of course, even that was helping him.

None of the women had seen him. He had spoken to them, occasionally, but what was in a voice? No one could identify him this way. They would have to find him first.

His hand tightened around the handle of his pickax, and he stared towards the large house, watching as the woman moved along the windows. She paused for a moment, her gray curls shifting as she reached for the hem of a curtain and began to tug it closed.

She couldn't see him, sitting in the car, watching her.

Empty of soul.

That was how he had always seen her. Soulless. Now, eighty years old, the woman had lived a selfish life. A life that had caused so much pain to so many. In a way, he wasn't the real monster.

The real monsters hid behind white picket fences and under dazzling chandeliers.

She was a soulless witch, and he was going to kill her last.

It had taken him nearly fifty years to find the right moment.

Carl was dying, after all.

But this woman, this particular stain, would be his final gift to the Pacific Northwest. And then the police would make him rich. And then he would leave this country forever, searching for greener pastures. He had once read about a killer in South America who was rumored to have murdered hundreds.

He smiled at the thought.

One day they would be writing books about him.

And who knew? If that time came, he might even be willing to discuss the years he had spent with the Ghost-killer as the mentor of the notorious murderer. And then, if he was feeling particularly frisky, he might even tell everything he knew about Artemis Blythe.

The lights flicked off in the dining room; the curtains had closed. And the woman without a soul disappeared from sight.

She lived alone. The empty lots on either side of her would be of no help either. He smirked as he pushed out of the front seat of his car, climbing rope clutched in one hand, his pickax in the other.

And even now, the police were helping him. He could hear the helicopter blades in the sky, only a couple of miles away. The sounds, the distraction of neighbors tuned into news stations, would help disguise any noise he made. Or, perhaps, more accurately, the noises *she* was bound to make.

No one would hear her scream.

CHAPTER 14

Morning came in the form of lancing sunlight through the front window of the car, and Artemis winced against the glare. Forester was driving again. Wade seemed satisfied to sit in the passenger seat, studying his phone.

"What else?" Forester was saying.

Artemis tried to listen, but the lack of sleep from the night before, the few hours she'd managed to snatch in her new place, and the knots her stomach had twisted in the entire night, had left her somewhat distracted.

Her mind kept slipping back to that cold, dirty, terrified woman in the dark. The horror of the situation Artemis had found her in. The fear the woman had exuded.

She had run away, hadn't she?

In a way, now, Artemis wanted to find this prolific murderer even more. If only to confirm he hadn't come back and snatched the woman she'd rescued.

A runaway Artemis could deal with. Maybe Forester was right—maybe she'd run home...

Artemis sighed, trying not to let her head spin. Mr. Arthur still hadn't confessed. In fact, from Wade's report, he hadn't said much of anything, except for the word *lawyer.*

He was somehow involved. No remorse, no regret. No grief over the thought of dead women or victims trapped in metal boxes. If anything, he'd only seemed scared at the Watkins family name.

But as she'd realized the night before, the only path forward involved Sierra—the survivor from the mineshaft. And also, she'd realized, the *second* woman who'd survived being locked in the shed. The search party leader had mentioned the second survivor was also being sent to the nearest hospital—which was the same one Sierra had been taken to.

"What else?" Forester repeated, louder.

Wade grunted and glanced over. "Umm... Sixty-five distinct victims," he said. "All of them killed either by suffocation, dehydration or wounds created by that same odd, curved weapon."

"Hmm. Ages?"

"Women, generally. A couple of men. Youngest woman was in her late teens. Oldest was in her fifties."

Artemis perked up now. "Wait," she said suddenly, trying to catch up to a conversation she'd refrained from participating in up to this point. "The coroner's report is in?"

Wade shot a look over the shoulder of his seat while Forester sped up the highway.

"Yeah," Wade said slowly. "Dr. Bryant sent it this morning. Weren't you listening?"

"Umm, no. Sorry. Mind saying it again?"

"Which part?"

"Umm... The youngest victim was a late teenager?" Artemis could feel her heart pounding. Helen had been fifteen when she disappeared. Granted, the killer might have kept her for a bit at first—as horrible as the thought was. She shifted the question and frowned, "Actually—wait. Do we have DNA? Anything?"

"A few of them are too old. Long before any sort of DNA was being commonly used," Wade said in his monotone. The man shrugged. "But a few others we know were local prostitutes. One was a widow from two towns over. Another was a bachelorette from California."

Forester glared through the windshield. "Single women, widows and prostitutes. The bastard is a sick twist... I still think Jeb Arthur is involved."

"Too young," Artemis and Wade said.

"Look at you two on the same page. I don't give a shit if he's too young. Maybe he had a partner. Or a mentor. Either way, the guy is guilty as sin, and you know it. He's a creep."

"Doesn't mean he's a murderer," Artemis murmured. For some reason, she thought of Tommy, her brother. He had the same mismatched eyes as her and the same troubling family history. He was a criminal, but he wasn't anything like their father.

"I don't think Mr. Arthur is the murderer," Artemis said quietly.

"Why not?"

"He's too stupid."

Forester smirked. Wade chuckled.

"No, I mean it. That trick, lowering your gun then shoving his shotgun? He fell for it. When you took him in for questioning, all that thrashing about, yelling—he exhausted himself. That was *not* a man in control."

Even as she said it, she pictured her own father, sitting calm and collected back at the prison. The way he played emotions, the way he postured. Control was important to narcissists. At least, the perception of control. And she couldn't think of anything *less* self-controlled than Mr. Arthur's display in the police station hallway.

"I mean..." she hesitated. "Obviously, I don't know for certain. It's a guess... but a good guess," she added quickly. "He's too young. He's too uncontrolled. Plus, his speech pattern was completely different from the one on the phone."

"What about that woman you found—our little runaway," Forester said.

"We don't know she ran away."

"She wasn't kidnapped again, Artemis. Either Mr. Arthur is our guy, or the real killer was miles away, keeping well clear."

Artemis winced at the jolt in her gut. She adjusted her seat belt, sighing. "I hope you're right," she said simply. "But if I was a betting person, I'd say Arthur isn't our killer. Too young and too brash. He might be involved. Might even have helped bury the bodies, but we're looking for someone else."

"That's a guess."

"Yes. It is. Don't forget, though—we have a third woman out there still in need of our help."

Forester shivered visibly, shaking his head in quick, jerking motions. "This whole thing gives me the creeps. Locking them in those boxes like that? That's messed up."

"Evil," Wade said simply.

Artemis nodded at both sentiments. "I think... I think we should find out if the Watkins family has any members nearby. I haven't been able to find much about them."

"You think they're involved?"

"They own the land," Artemis said. "They might have had access to Jeb's phone number from two years ago. Especially if it was a work phone. They own the ranch. They own the mountain where all those bodies were found."

"Good point. Wade—wanna look them up?"

"After," Wade shot back. "We're here."

He was pointing through the windshield towards a large, blue-and-white, glass building rising out of the ground on the other side of an off ramp.

In response, Forester gunned the engine, veering in front of two cars, chattering about hospital food as the vehicles blared their horns.

***

Artemis peered into the hospital room where Sierra sat propped up in her bed. The woman was shivering, and a long, white bandage was wrapped over her arm where the phone number tattoo had been displayed earlier.

Forester and Wade stood behind her, both of them goading her on. Wade did so silently, using only glances and urgent nods.

Forester took a more direct approach. "Come on, Checkers. This is what you're here for. You're our chatterer. Go chat."

Artemis blinked, glanced back and frowned. "First of all," she whispered, "insensitive. Secondly, you're the chatty one. I'm more... *stoic.*"

"Stoic? That a type of steroid?"

"What? No." She sighed and tried to protest as Forester gave her a little push through the hospital door.

Artemis spotted one of the nurses who'd escorted them to the private room watching in disapproval down the hall.

But Artemis stepped into the room nonetheless, putting on a professional expression. Not that she really knew what one was. Her experience, across the table from some genius who'd recently memorized an old opening in order to trick her, was usually one that involved poker-faces and dour glances.

So instead, she tried to smile.

The expression didn't fit, so as she stepped across the squeaky, tiled floor, she shifted to something more like a polite, inquisitive look.

As she drew near, Sierra glanced up.

The woman was shivering on the hospital bed, only a thin, flimsy blanket covering her form. Artemis took another hesitant step forward then went still.

Her eyes were moving quickly, her mind doubly so. She took in the woman's hunched posture. Noticed the way the left hand curled over the hem of the blanket. Noticed how the bandage was only thin gauze, but there was no sign of blood or injury, nor any favoring of the other arm.

This, Artemis guessed, meant the bandage was there simply to hide the phone number tattoo.

Which also meant, the woman had likely requested this favor.

For a woman to request anything, she had to be at least *capable* of stringing coherent sentences together. All of this compiled in one culminating thought; the woman sitting on the bed remembered *some* things.

At least enough to cover the hated tattoo.

And so it was from this place of expecting both coherency and a form of recollection that Artemis started. She began with a name.

"Hello, Sierra."

The woman flinched, glanced up, then down again. Her features were no longer strained. Artemis' gaze moved past Sierra towards the second bed beyond a dividing foam board. The second woman who'd been discovered last night was resting on this bed. Artemis could just discern the woman's head, on a pillow.

Technically, they weren't cleared yet by hospital staff to speak with the other woman. But Forester and Wade were both watching from the door, standing back as she'd request-ed, keeping to the shadows to avoid an overt intrusive pres-ence.

"My name is Artemis. I was wondering if I could ask you a few questions."

"I d-don't know anything..."

The woman's small voice broke Artemis' heart. She closed her eyes, exhaling briefly. But pressed on. "I'm sure you think that. But... maybe I can help you remember."

Another small voice. "I don't want to remember."

"I understand."

Artemis swallowed, shifting from foot to foot. She shot a look back towards the agents. Forester was making a shooing motion with his hands as if to say *get on with it.* Wade just frowned, arms crossed over his impressive pectorals.

Artemis turned back.

"Sierra, I called the number on your arm."

She flinched.

"Do you know who gave you that tattoo?"

"Y-yes."

"Who?"

"Please... I'm... I'm tired."

Artemis went quiet, wondering if she ought to just turn and walk away. This all felt so cruel. She wondered, if she'd been able to cry, if she might have in that moment. But all she felt was anxiety, guilt... secondhand pain.

"My sister was killed in those mountains," Artemis said. She didn't even realize she was speaking those words until they erupted from her lips. Normally so collected, so analytical, Artemis wasn't one accustomed to leveraging personal pain too often... But it was as she said it that Artemis realized she *wasn't* using it for any sort of leverage. She was simply stating a fact.

A fact that mattered to her.

Sierra glanced up. "Oh."

"It was years ago," Artemis said simply.

"Did... did *he* kill her?"

"I don't know. So it was a he?"

"No."

"You said he."

"Well..." The blanket bunched around her hand, and she shifted her legs. A long sigh followed. "I... I think it was a he. His voice was deep. He was very aggressive."

"Did you see him."

130

"No!"

"Sorry. I don't mean to upset you."

"I couldn't see. He knocked me out at a truck stop."

"Which stop?"

"Twenty-three. Near Sajuwan."

Artemis glanced back and noticed Wade quickly texting the information into his phone. Forester just watched from the shadows.

"Anything else?"

"No..."

"What type of car did he drive?"

"I don't know. Umm. A truck."

Artemis gave a quick nod and a smile. "You're doing very well. Thank you. What type of truck?"

"I don't know."

"What color?"

"It was dark; I don't know!"

Artemis held up a placating hand. "I'm sorry," she said. Then, as if she couldn't help herself, she added, "This is my first real case... At least, the first time I'm supposed to be doing this." Artemis sighed. "I don't... don't know how to speak with people who've been..." She trailed off again, wincing and wishing she'd just stuck to the script she'd rehearsed in her mind.

"Broken?"

"What? No. I don't mean that."

"Then what? I... I think I'm broken," she whispered. "I can't get his voice out of my head. It was so cold..."

Artemis wanted to lean in, to give the woman's hand a quick squeeze. But she felt as if she'd found herself in a play with no script. She didn't know how to act. So instead she patted the foot of the bed, staying well clear of the woman's own foot, which was a lump under the blankets.

"I... I was attacked by a killer too," Artemis said slowly. "In a hotel room. He nearly drowned me."

The woman's eyes widened, and she looked up for the first time, staring at Artemis. "Really? When?"

"Only a month ago."

Those wide eyes brightened. "A *month*? And you're... you're..." she trailed off.

"I'm doing alright," said Artemis simply.

The translation played through her mind. *I can't cry. I don't know if I love anyone. I'm mildly attracted to a sociopath. I'm trying to meet up with a man whose father was killed in front of me. My brother is a criminal. My sister is probably dead, but I won't admit it. My father is a mass murderer. I haven't been on a real date in nearly two decades...*

But saying any of this would have taken more courage than she'd managed to amass. And so she gave a quick, encouraging nod, lying with a smile.

"You'll be fine too," she said. In for a penny in for a pound. "I promise."

The woman relaxed a bit at this, still watching Artemis as if seeking any note of deception.

And again, Artemis lied. This time with her facial structure. Using body language to communicate an untruth.

How very, very much like her father.

The thought repulsed her so much, she quickly said, "Is there anything else you remember? Anything at all?"

"Umm... No. Well... I heard sizzling."

"Sizzling?"

"Mhmm."

"Like cooking?"

"No. Like in a jar."

"A jar?"

"I heard him open and close lids. My mother used to make jams. It was the same sound. When he opened lids, I heard sizzling."

Artemis wrinkled her nose. "Oh."

A voice suddenly echoed from behind the partition. "It was acid."

Artemis glanced over sharply. The head of the second woman—whom they were technically forbidden from speaking with until her fluids had stabilized—was now sitting propped up. Her expression was nonexistent.

Her eyes hollow, her face gaunt.

Artemis stared at this woman. "I—I'm Artemis."

"I heard."

"And you?"

"None of your business."

Artemis winced. "I see."

"I was in that shed for three days, you know. You guys took your time about it."

There was a clear note of bitterness to this second woman's voice. Sierra had gone quiet now, allowing the conversation to shift.

Artemis said, "You think the sound was acid?"

"Yes."

"You're sure?"

"Yes."

"How?"

"Because," the woman said simply with a shrug. "I spotted a large, white bottle marked with pH."

"Are you a chemist?"

A snort. "I took high school chemistry before dropping out. I'm observant. He knew you."

"Excuse me?"

"Your name. He knew your name."

"Artemis?"

"Yes."

"What do you mean?"

"He was excited you were on the phone. He asked me about you—asked if I knew you as if he was hoping I had."

Artemis frowned now, crossing her arms. "Did he say anything else?"

"Not that I can think of."

"Did you see him?"

"No. I was blindfolded. Only saw the acid thing because it was under a table." The woman scowled, her gaunt features arranging into a deep frown. "That's when he shoved me in that coffin. I thought I was dead. Guess not." She collapsed back on the pillow, sounding neither disappointed nor excited by this last comment.

"Umm... Is there anything else either of you..."

But the second woman had closed the drape again. Sierra was shaking her head in stiff motions. Artemis sighed.

The killer had *known* her. Been *excited* about her? Did that tell her anything new, or was it just old news?

"If... If ever I can do anything," Artemis said slowly. She glanced at Sierra. Then, quietly, so only she could hear, Artemis said, "You'll recover. If you want to—you will. I promise."

A strange claim, she realized. Not her usual fare, dealing in certainty and probability. But what did this claim cost her?

Many people recovered, didn't they? She had to believe it. Some might even have accused her of taking it on faith. Then again, some things had to be taken on faith. She thought of her brother, Tommy. Thought of her hope of finding Helen...

Still, as she said it, even Artemis believed it for a moment. And the look of excitement in the woman's eyes was reward enough.

Artemis shifted uncomfortably, wondering if she was expected to press more, but before she could, Forester's voice barked sharply from the doorway.

"Blythe! Hey! Blythe!"

She turned quickly, frowning.

Wade was already jogging down the hall, moving fast. Forester's long leg had angled away from the door, suggesting he'd been in the middle of following Wade but stopped to call her.

Forester pointed at her, then gestured. "Another one. Hurry—we need to go!"

Artemis froze. "Another what?"

Forester eyed her. As sheer dread flooded her system.

"You coming? Checkers—*now!*" Forester turned on his heel and hastened towards the stairwell.

Chapter 15

Police sirens stirred the distant winds; blue and red flashed off the windows of the large, white-painted home. Artemis moved up the stairs, her legs heavy, her footsteps timid.

Forester stood in the doorway, right on the verge of a pool of blood, which had spilled under the door. This was what had alerted a jogger to the crime.

Artemis stared into the house, past crime-scene tape and multiple officers standing sentry.

A woman lay on a carpet—an old woman, motionless, her purple sweater now stained crimson. She'd been stabbed from behind. That much was obvious. Stabbed over and over again.

"Mrs. Watkins died late last night," A voice was saying.

Artemis turned sharply, looking towards where Agent Wade spoke with a young woman in a blue uniform. "Watkins?" Artemis called out.

The young policewoman and Wade both looked over. The officer frowned, but Wade murmured something, and the officer answered, "Isabel Watkins. She was eighty. Doesn't look like our killer took anything. We're trying to contact next of kin, but it's proving difficult." The cop addressed this last part to Wade.

Agent Wade nodded, emitting a frustrated sigh and taking quick notes on his phone. Artemis pulled her own phone out, scanning her most recent search history.

Watkins. Watkins mountain. Eleazar Watkins. Gold-mining Watkins land.

She'd tried nearly every variation she could, but nothing came up. On the way over, in the grim silence of the vehicle, Wade had put in an official request for all pertinent information on the Watkins family.

They were still waiting to hear back.

Apparently, wealth didn't just insulate people from prosecution, it could also insulate them from investigation.

"Wade, any more news on the Watkins family yet?" Artemis called out.

Wade glanced at her but shook his head. "We don't know if she's related to them," he replied. "Still waiting."

Artemis frowned. "Can't we just, you know—search the DMV or something?"

Wade shook his head. "Lot of people named Watkins. Deed of sale is listed to the estate. Only signatory is Jeb Arthur. Gonna have to wait for them to narrow it."

Artemis huffed in frustration, turning to look back into the house, trying not to stare at the body. Another corpse. The same puncture wounds as the other victims found in the mountain. What weapon was the killer using?

Not even Forester had a good guess yet.

Artemis sidled past Cameron, moving with a generous leap *over* the blood and into the house. A cop tried to protest, but she ignored him, passing a couple of cardigans dangling on a wooden hook by the door, and moving into the house.

The crime itself had seemed clear enough. Someone had broken in, murdered the old woman then left.

But that didn't mean there weren't clues to be found.

Especially in the home of someone named Watkins.

***

As Artemis moved through the dining room, she scanned the walls which were noticeably devoid of any photographs, or pictures. Artemis frowned, moving onto a bedroom, and peering into the top drawer. Socks and the like.

The next drawer. More cardigans.

She moved on to a closet, opening it wide and inhaling the odor of mothballs. Waving a hand in front of her face, Artemis sniffed a couple more times to clear her sinuses and then moved a few of the jackets on coat hangers. They rattled as they shifted.

Artemis frowned, peering up at a long wooden shelf. A couple of boxes. She grabbed these and pulled them down.

Only as she popped the lids did she think to consider the ethics of going through the private matters of a dead woman.

But the momentary affliction of conscience vanished quick enough. Artemis wasn't here to pry. She was here to stop a maniac.

She tossed the lids to the boxes.

In the first, she found shoes.

The second... empty.

Artemis huffed, turning back towards the closet, scanning once more.

Then, she dropped to her knees, peering under the bed, uncertain, even, what she was searching for. She found a loose sock. A ball of yarn… A small brown key for a jewelry box and a green straw.

Artemis leaned back on her haunches, frowning again.

She scanned the room once more, eyes searching.

Then she paused.

No jewelry box.

A key for one… but no box.

Artemis hesitated and then ducked, stretching her arm and sliding across a carpet that was in desperate need of a vacuum. She snagged the key. And then, she hesitated, glancing at the sock.

A very large, bulging sock. She grabbed this too, pulling it from under the bed, along with the key, and deposited both treasures onto the bed.

Artemis stared at the sock and the key, biting her lip. She lifted the sock, shook it a few times, and a small, rectangular box dropped onto the bed. A box with a keyhole.

Artemis felt her pulse quicken. She inserted the key into the slot and opened the box. As she stared into the confines of the small space, her brow furrowed even more deeply.

"What in the…" she trailed off, shaking her head.

Pictures… Very old, worn pictures. Children at play on wooden sawhorses in one. In another, the same children, older now, splashing in a river. The next photo was of a dour, frowning family, looking away from a small, wooden-framed house.

In fact, she recognized the house. More accurately, she recognized the barn behind it. In this photo, though, the barn wasn't tilted.

Artemis placed the three photos on the bed, studying them. She flipped them over, scanning the backs. One read: *Eli, Desi, Carl.*

The other read. *Desi, Carl, Eli.*

Artemis shook her head, murmuring the names to herself. Desi. Carl. Eli.

What did it mean? The woman's last name was Watkins. And she kept these pictures in a locked box, hidden under her bed.

But why?

Fear?

Privacy?

Who had killed Ms. Watkins last night? Who was behind the murder of sixty-five others on the mountain slopes? Artemis shook her head, glancing over her shoulder as she pocketed the photos.

It was as she looked towards the door that she spotted the message.

Written in blood, hidden behind the wooden door so only someone who'd entered the room and closed it would see.

The words, painted in blood, simply read, *Soulless witch.*

Artemis exhaled, staring at the door, feeling a prickle along her back. None of this was adding up. Something else was at play. Something she couldn't quite figure out. She took a hesitant step towards the bloody letters.

Empty of a soul.

Was this the third piece of the riddle?

So why was the killer *giving* her answers? What was he playing at? *Why* was he playing a game with the police after all these years?

As these questions swirled and Artemis stared at the blood on the wall, her phone began to vibrate. Her hand darted into her pocket, and she lifted the device.

For a moment, she had half hoped to recognize Jamie Kramer's number.

But now, as she stared, her stomach twisted.

Unknown Caller.

Her eyes bounced to the bloody words, her hand touched absentmindedly at the photos in her pocket. Desi, Eli and Carl Watkins? Perhaps the names would help narrow Wade's search. Or at least remove some obstacles insulating the Watkins estate.

One thing was certain, whether or not Jeb Arthur was involved, his employers certainly had something to do with all of this.

The phone continued to ring. And so Artemis paused, considered her words carefully and lifted the device, answering swiftly.

"Carl Watkins?" she guessed, without missing a beat.

And then she waited quietly, skin prickling, for the response.

CHAPTER 16

A soft chuckle emanated from the other line. "Carl Watkins?" the voice said. "Hmm. Someone's fishing, aren't they?"

Artemis scowled across the room, facing the bloody letters on the wall. It was the same lilting voice, disguised by some audio trick. She pictured the woman downstairs, lying in blood. Pictured the terror in the eyes of the two women recovering at the hospital.

She stood there, frozen to the old carpet. Off to her right, a window displayed the dance of red and blue lights. The wail of distant sirens continued their rapid approach. Artemis tried to keep herself calm. She didn't bother fetching Forester this time.

Tracking the number hadn't worked before.

"Why are you calling me?"

Another chuckle. "Do you know why they call me the Professor?"

"Who's *they*?"

"My students, of course. I've taken some, over the years... And you, Artemis Blythe. You are a very peculiar woman."

Artemis frowned now. "How do you know me?"

"How couldn't I? Everyone knows the Ghost-killer's daughter. Well... at least, everyone of a certain persuasion in these parts."

"That's not what I was told. I was told you *knew* me. How? Have we met?"

"Tut-tut. Now we're fishing again, see?"

"Are you a Watkins?"

"Who?"

"You're pretending like you don't know whose land you buried corpses on for three decades?"

"*Oh Watkins?* Yes... yes, rings a bell."

"Why did you kill Mrs. Watkins?"

"Who said I did?"

"She was killed in her home. The same weapon you used on half the victims in the mountain."

"Artemis, I really am enjoying myself. But I have to go. Would you like another riddle?"

Artemis felt a flicker of dread. The idea of racing to find more women before they were killed made her stomach churn. But also, this opened up a line of questioning she'd intended.

Cautiously, Artemis cleared her throat. She paused, shifting on the soft carpet. Then she said, "We found that woman in the mineshaft. Found the next two victims. That's three women we saved from you."

It was a risky ask. But Artemis was, indeed, fishing. If the killer *knew* that the woman from the basement wasn't in police custody, then it meant he might very well have done something with her. But if he conceded the point, that meant that the woman from the night before had simply run away. Artemis' conscience couldn't bear up under the first eventuality.

And so it was with great relief that she heard him sneer, "Three survived. But many others have been emptied of life."

A flicker of relief. He didn't seem to know anything about the runaway. Artemis said, "What is it with you and *emptying*?"

"Now that would be telling, Ms. Blythe. Would you like to hear my riddle or not?" A pause. "Well?"

"I'm thinking," Artemis replied, her skin still crawling. She frowned now, hesitant. "Why now?" she said slowly. "Why after all these years? Why play your games *now*? Why not stick to the shadows, hiding, committing your murders without being discovered?"

No response this time. Then, an angrier voice, "Do you want the riddle? Or should I just kill them?"

"I don't need your riddle," Artemis said quietly.

"Their blood will be on your hands."

"Are you Eli Watkins?"

"You're still fishing. You know what, change of plans, you like the Watkins family so much?" And then he hung up.

She stood there, shivering, feeling a sudden dread. She had made the right call, hadn't she?

He was playing with them. And by participating, they were helping. She didn't know how or what with, but she knew that they were participating in whatever sick machinations this killer had come up with. He called himself the Professor and suggested he had students. But what exactly did that mean?

She shook her head, scowling as she did. There were two strands of curiosity. But she would pursue them one at a time.

She lowered her phone, turned to the door, and hastened back through.

She needed to find the others. They needed that information on the Watkins family.

Somehow, the killer was connected to them. The woman downstairs attested to that. The killer's reaction also testified as much. Somehow, an ultra-wealthy family with deep roots in the land were involved with a decades-old serial killer. And the only way she could think to find out how was to ask them.

CHAPTER 17

Artemis didn't tell the agents about the phone call, but as they pulled up the long, winding driveway just north of Seattle, she wondered if she'd made a mistake.

But no... No, the killer was playing games. Artemis made a living doing that very thing. By constantly bringing up the Watkins family, she'd managed to antagonize the killer. It was like tossing chum to a shark.

At the very least, she knew where his attention was directed.

Or... maybe the killer *was* a Watkins, pretending otherwise.

Time would tell.

That was... if they reached the enormous estate in a timely fashion. The driveway, lined with hedges and colorful perennials, seemed to go on for miles.

It was as they turned a bend, trundling slowly along the smooth road, dipping from behind a thick, dark line of freshly planted trees, that a faint, collective inhale took the car.

All three of them stared up the driveway towards the scene beyond. The estate wasn't what Artemis had been expecting. The house itself was small; clean, neat, ranch-style with a converted garage boasting a vaulted ceiling.

But the land itself was...

Idyllic.

A large lake led to small ponds. Small ponds led to streams that culminated in water features of stone, marble and moss. Resplendent flowers, the redolence tingeing the air, ornamented the water features. Tulip gardens encircled the ponds. And the lake was adorned in willow trees and blue flowers.

Horses ran wild in fenced-in acreage. Cattle took shelter in a second paddock, gathered by a water trough, under the shadow of a wide-branched tree—which looked foreign to the area, suggesting it had been specially imported and cultivated.

Forester whistled slowly as he pulled the car alongside one of the water features. Multiple stone arches were stacked on top of each other like a miniature Roman aqueduct. Vines draped on either side, tangled leaves extending towards the water.

Artemis stared as they passed, feeling almost transported in an otherworldly sense. Their vehicle trundled past, still moving slowly, and Artemis spotted strangely hued birds moving in the trees. Off to the right, she heard the faint hum of bees.

"You're sure this is the right place?" she murmured.

Agent Wade grunted. "Only place that showed up on the report," he said. "An Elison Watkins lives here with his family."

Elison. *Eli.* Artemis frowned, her hand moving to the photograph she'd squirreled into her pocket. She still wasn't quite sure *why* the latest victim had hidden the photo beneath the bed. She also didn't know what to make of the killer's cryptic threat about the Watkins.

"Let's hurry," Artemis said, feeling a prickle of anxiety. "We need to speak with Mr. Watkins. Now."

Forester shot her a curious glance, but Wade just nodded. The two FBI agents returned their gaze to the small ranch house at the top of the idyllic scene. They moved hastily, driving fast. Artemis leaned against the door, one hand tap-tap-tapping.

As they pulled into the driveway, the smooth road gave way to an equally well-kept, asphalt parking area. A couple of other cars were visible outside the doors to the garage. One of them looked like a spaceship to Artemis.

Forester stared at the red and pink thing, whistling. "Didn't know they'd already released the new Lambo. Shit—she's pretty."

Wade didn't even glance at the car. He pushed out of their own vehicle as Forester pulled to a stop and began moving directly towards the door. Artemis followed. Forester lingered in the parking lot to check out the fancy car, running his hands along the hood.

Artemis' attention turned to the ranch house. It was difficult for her to know *what* they were looking for. The killer had been active on the Watkins' land for decades. The killer had just murdered Mrs. Watkins—though they still hadn't quite determined the woman's connection to the owners of the Wishing Well property and all its empty mineshafts.

This, she decided, would be a good place to start.

That was until the side door kicked open. A snarling voice erupted, "Get away from my car!" Two figures emerged. Both of them looking as if they'd been raised on a steady diet of gummy bears and steroids. Their bellys extended over leather belts, but their arms bulged with muscles.

The two men had neat, combed hair and hooded eyes. In fact, as they emerged from the side of the house, Artemis realized they were twins. Evident in their matching, narrowed eyes, upturned noses and the overall supercilious tilt of their chins. They carried themselves like bar room brawlers but dressed like trust-fund sucklers.

The first twin, almost as tall as Forester but with a beer gut like a church bell, was pointing his finger towards the agent. "Get off my car."

"Hey! Hey! Watch it!" Wade barked, hurrying past Artemis, around the side of the house to come to his partner's defense.

Forester raised his hands in mock surrender, stepping back from the spaceship. "My bad," he said. "Just checking. Nice ride." He gave a quick, charming smile which usually worked on folks.

But the twins weren't having it. "Who the hell are you?" snapped the original speaker.

The second twin hadn't said a word yet, but he lingered behind his brother with a quiet glare. "Who?" said Forester. "Well, let's calm down. I'm Cam."

"Cam?"

Wade sighed, stepping in between the two men. "He's *Agent* Forester."

"Oh, yeah," Cam said, "That too."

"Agent? What type of agent?" asked the big fellow.

The other man was scowling deeply now. Something had changed. A tension settled over them. Artemis wasn't sure what to make of it. The two men were now glaring at Forester and Wade. One of them was reaching slowly towards his back pocket.

"Hey now," Forester said, pointing, his own hand lowering slightly. "Keep your hands where I can see them, alright? It's a bit of a fetish I have."

"Think you're funny, *Cam?*" the speaker twin snapped.

Artemis took a step back, along the side of the house, watching with a grimace. And then, the twin said something that made her pause.

"We got the call about you," he said. "*Agent.* Right. Think we're stupid?"

"Yes," Forester replied, nodding earnestly.

"Shut up," Wade whispered.

Forester pointed at his partner. "I think he wants you guys to be quiet. Now how about we get a couple of names?"

"Nah," murmured the first twin, eyes hooded. "He said you'd come by. Said you'd pretend to be agents. You're the bastards who wasted Nana!"

Now, Forester went still. Artemis had seen this transition before. It was clinically impossible for Forester to take most things seriously. To him, teasing, mocking, playing was his version of conversing. But sometimes, when he sensed danger, there was a bit of a change.

It was in the eyes first. Moving from twinkling amusement to a sudden cold. Also in the shoulders. A relaxed, easy-going posture suddenly going rigid and then relaxing once more but with the ease of a fighter in a cage.

It was also in the narrowing of his lips, pressing tightly together for a brief moment as if holding back some comment.

One moment, Forester had the bearing and look of a class clown in a suit. The next, he looked like a killer. The transition in his eyes, especially, sent a shiver up Artemis' spine.

Forester was studying the two men now, the humor having bled from his voice like water through sand. "Now, let's hang on a moment, gentlemen. I'm not sure who you've been talking to. But we haven't wasted *anyone.* At least, not recently. And we *are* FBI. Just let me reach for my badge, okay?"

But the two men didn't notice the change in Forester's tone. Didn't seem to see the transition in his posture.

Artemis was quickly trying to track what was being said. Someone had placed a call. *He said you'd say that.* The killer. It must have been. They'd been talking to someone who'd told them that Forester and Wade were coming. Someone who'd had the Watkins family number. And had enough trust, or information, in order to make them angry.

By the sound of things, the killer had kept good on his promise. Not a riddle, but revenge. Artemis hadn't played his game, so the killer had played hers... and by the look of things, he'd kicked the hornet's nest good and hard.

The twins were both glaring. The one in the lead murmured, "I saw a picture of what you sickos did to Nana."

The second twin was nodding determinedly.

"She was eighty, you bastard!" With the sudden eruption of temper, the man howled in rage and swung hard. His fist flew through the air, scything towards Forester's head. The second man howled, yanking the weapon he'd been reaching for from his holster.

But Wade was already moving. Also having tracked the weapon, Wade darted forward, fast. The well-built agent slammed into the belly of the big twin.

The gun he'd pulled went flying into the manicured lawn by the house. Meanwhile, Agent Wade brought the larger man down to the ground in a pile of flailing limbs and feet. Wade and the twin struggled desperately with grunts and gasps of exertion to try and gain the upper hand. Wade's fingers found the man's throat. But the silent twin gouged at Wade's eyes. The agent was forced to release his grip and shift, but the switch in posture gave the far larger man an opportunity to buck his hips, throwing Wade off.

The two men tussled, rolling in the grass.

Meanwhile, Agent Forester had avoided the punch from the second twin.

"Come on now," Forester was saying, stepping back, hands out in surrender. "Cut it out, boys. We're not who you thin—"

The second punch caught him in the chin and sent him reeling. Artemis yelled. Forester hit the ground *hard.* As he turned, scrambling on the tarmac, he pressed a hand to his lip, pulling it away and revealing blood. Forester's eyes flashed and a grin stretched his face. "Alright then," he muttered.

Forester's attacker was trying to kick the fallen man in the head, but now, still grinning, Cameron surged to his feet, caught the leg deftly and sent two quick punches to the man's belly. The big guy gasped, the air whooshing from his lungs. "Ah, come on, bud—you want to do this? Let's do it right."

Forester danced to the side, avoiding another wild haymaker. He closed the distance again, as quick as lightning; two more punches, this time to the other side of the big guy's ribs. But before the twin could lash out, Forester darted back again. He was now clicking his tongue, shaking his head. "Fists up, man. Up. Look, see this? Don't put your knuckles to your cheek. If I hit your hand, I'll knock you out." Forester was still giving pointers as he ducked another blow. "Yeah, see, there you go—give it a bit of a gap. Ready for a kick? Here we go."

Forester's foot lashed out, catching the attacker in the gut. A loud whooshing noise erupted from the well-dressed twin. He doubled over, gasping at the ground, spit trailing. Forester took a step towards him, patting him on the back, avoiding a grasping hand. "No cardio, bud."

Artemis just watched, stunned. She knew Forester had been a professional cage fighter. She'd also heard about a time when he'd been in the cage, had his arm broken, and after a few minutes, he'd knocked his opponent out with his *other* arm. Sometimes, with all the teasing, the playful irreverence and the like, she forgot *who* she was dealing with.

"Hey Wade, mind if I borrow the second?"

Agent Wade was currently struggling under the sheer girth of his attacker. The big man was reaching for his gun, which had forced Wade to go for the extended arm. But this also allowed the silent twin to start punching Wade in the kidney. By the third blow, Wade was emitting a pained wheezing sound.

Forester waited patiently. "Please?" he added, standing next to his own opponent, who was still bent double, gasping at the ground, while peering down at his struggling partner.

"Cam, asshole!" were the only words Wade managed.

"I'll take that as a yes."

Forester then reached down, looped his hand through the belt of the second attacker and ripped him bodily off his partner, pulling him towards the car. This second man began swiping at Forester now. Encouraged by his brother's attacks, the first twin also straightened, coming towards Cameron.

Artemis wasn't sure if she ought to do something. She glanced at the gun which the twin had dropped. Wade was struggling to his feet, grunting and clutching at his kidney.

But Forester didn't seem to want... or need the help. He was busy fighting the two brutes. A couple of punches landed, but whenever this happened, Cameron only released a loud laugh as if it were the funniest thing in the world to him.

Whenever one of the twins tried to collect his breath, though, Forester would bury his fist into their stomachs or ribs. He never seemed to aim for the head. And like this, standing by the fancy sports car, Forester slowly whittled down the two men.

After a bit, Forester, breathing heavily, murmured, "Had enough?"

Neither twin responded. Both were gasping heavily. Both bruised and hurt. Artemis was still frozen by the porch, watching the whole scene in horror. Suddenly, seeming to decide he wanted no further part in this dance with the fighter, the silent twin turned, glancing from Wade to Artemis with red-stained eyes, and then he lunged towards her.

Artemis yelped. Forester lunged and caught the man by his belt, dragging him back.

"Nope," Cameron said simply.

The other brother took another shot at Forester. But this time, Forester seemed to have remembered there were others nearby. The moment the brute had gone for Artemis, something like recognition flickered in his gaze. Something even like... guilt.

Instead of playing with his food, Forester jerked the big man back and brought an elbow into his temple. He followed it up with a straight right to the second man's skull.

Both of them hit the ground simultaneously, flopping on the floor, unconscious at Forester's feet.

Cameron exhaled a few times, wiped some sweat off his forehead and then wiped his hand on the fleece sweater of one of his attackers. Then, sheepishly, he glanced at Artemis. "Sorry," he muttered.

She didn't respond, just stared.

Wade, who had recovered the discarded firearm, rubbed ruefully at his ribs. "Hey, Cam," he said.

"Yeah, bud?"

"Next time I'm getting pummeled, you don't need my permission to beat up the guy, kay?"

Forester nodded and flashed a thumbs up. "Didn't want to be greedy is all."

Wade just shook his head, spat off to the side, the saliva stained with red, and then, tucking the discarded gun into his waistband, he turned towards the ranch house again.

Artemis realized the reason for his sudden attention.

A third figure had emerged in the doorway. This figure wasn't carrying a weapon, nor did she look ready to bum-rush FBI agents. She was, perhaps, middle-aged—the same age as Cynthia Washington—and was frowning severely at the scene in the parking lot.

She wore a bathrobe and slippers. Her hair was a mess, and yet somehow, she still communicated an air of authority. It was in the posture, in the eyes, in the glare. She scanned the driveway, hissed in frustration, and scowled. Forester was already waving his badge about, as if worried he wouldn't have the chance to show it this time.

The woman took this in as well. She smoothed the front of her bathrobe, rubbed the sleep from her eyes and then said, with a sigh. "Why, may I ask, did you just knock out my sons?"

She didn't frown, didn't scowl. Her tone held no emotion. She simply stated the question matter-of-factly, then glanced at the three figures in her driveway, waiting patiently for an answer.

Artemis took in the woman's posture, the vacant look in her eyes. Bloodshot gaze, dilated pupils. This woman was clearly on something. Something quite powerful, given her calm reaction to the pummeling of her children. Forester and Wade shared a knowing glance, and Artemis suspected they'd reached a similar conclusion. Forester was massaging his knuckles while Wade took a step forward, still rubbing his ribs.

"Mrs. Watkins?" Wade said.

"Yes?"

Artemis stepped forward suddenly. "Do you know an Eli Watkins?"

The woman in the door glanced at Artemis, but it took her a moment to swivel her head, as if she were somehow moving in slow motion. After a second, her lips curled into a smile, and she nodded. "My brother Eli... yes. What about him?"

"He's your brother?"

"Well, brother-in-law. I married Carl."

Two of the names from the photograph. Artemis hesitated, then said. "Is your family related to Isabel Watkins?" She pictured the elderly woman lying in a pool of blood.

At the name, though, the first look of irritation crossed the woman's face. "We don't speak. Or... well, didn't." The woman sighed, passing a hand over her face and closing her eyes briefly, as if gathering herself. "From what I hear," she said slowly, swallowing and wetting her lips with her tongue, "Izzie was killed last night."

"Yes," Artemis said. She glanced at the two men at Forester's feet. One was starting to move. "Your boys mentioned they received a phone call from someone telling them that Isabel's killers were coming here. Do you know who that call was from?"

"Hmm—what? How horrible. No, dear, I was sleeping. Now... what is this about?" Her gaze landed on her unconscious boys, blinked and then her eyes suddenly widened. She began to frown, once again in slow motion, but Artemis interrupted before the woman's drug-addled mind could settle on anger.

"And who is Desi Watkins?"

"Desi? Oh, Desiree? My husband's sister. She died young, though. Really, I must insist—what is this about?"

Artemis stood there for a moment, trying to piece it together. The two goons at Forester's feet were hardly the subtle sort. To consider they'd conducted a murder operation for decades didn't seem right. Mrs. Watkins was high—a frail, small thing. Plus, the two victims at the hospital had insisted the voice of their captor had been male.

"Does anyone else live here, ma'am?" Artemis murmured.

"Yes, my husband, Carl. I told you."

"And where is he?"

"He isn't doing well."

"What do you mean?"

"I mean that," Watkins said, her voice bitter. "He's upstairs. In bed."

"May we see him?"

"If you must... but he just returned from the hospital. He's not exactly in a speaking mood."

Artemis blinked. "The hospital?"

"Yes," he is recovering from cancer. The moment she said it, though, she bit her lip and glanced off to the side. She sighed slowly, and her eyes filled with grief. "No... No, that's not true. Carl is dying. I know it." She sniffed and leaned her head back. "We all know it."

Now the two twins were sitting upright, both nursing their injuries and glaring at Forester. Meanwhile, Cameron had snagged Wade's cuffs and was busy securing the twins' arms behind their backs. "Just sit still for a bit," Forester muttered. "No harm, no foul."

Artemis turned to them though. Wade beat her to the question. "Who called you?" Wade said simply.

The spokesperson for the two glared from his mean little eyes, but then, glancing at his mother and then at Forester, he seemed to realize that he'd overestimated the newcomers' murderous tendencies. He gave a little huff of air and muttered something.

"I said, who called you?" Wade asked, his voice firm.

"Dunno," the guy said sullenly.

"What was the number?" Forester asked, leaning in and giving a little pat to the back of the big man's head.

The twin snarled, twisting and trying to escape Forester's hand. But at another insistent glare from Wade, he said, "Library. The old one dad built."

"A library called you?" Wade continued.

"Yeah."

"You said they mentioned we were here to harm you."

"They warned us you killed Nana."

The woman in the door scowled. "Don't call her that," she snapped. "Don't ever let me hear you call her that again."

Artemis glanced at the woman. "Isabel Watkins? She's this nana?"

"No," snapped the woman. "Isabel Watkins was my husband's mother. She was never a very kind woman. She wrote all of us out of the family will, in fact."

Artemis blinked. She glanced at Forester. Usually, motives weren't volunteered so quickly.

Forester cleared his throat and raised a hand as if he were in class. "So your husband is the sole benefactor of... what exactly?"

"All of it," said Mrs. Watkins. She spread her arms, indicating the land around them. Waving a hand airily towards the cars. "It's all *theirs*. Isabel. She left it to Carl."

"Hang on," Artemis said. "Only Carl? Your husband. I thought you said he had a brother."

"Eli?" Watkins shook her head. "He's not getting a penny. Like the rest of us. Isabel cut him off."

"Why?"

The woman shrugged. "Can't say I know, exactly." She hesitated, eyes narrowed. "What are you accusing us of? You haven't been reading those nasty tabloids, have you? Not a word of truth."

Artemis only remembered reading that blog page with news clippings from the 1850s. The news itself hadn't painted the Watkins family in a very favorable light. She decided, though, not to mention the blog.

"Back to this call from the library," Wade said, still frowning at the two men who'd assaulted the agents. "You just trusted the voice? Decided to start swinging at feds?"

"Nah," said the one twin. "Only dad's friends have the house number. No one else does."

"Friends and family?" Artemis asked suddenly.

They shrugged, nodding at her.

"Figured," the man said, "that one of the family friends was trying to warn us. We just wanted to protect you, mom!" He looked back at his mother, but her expression was vacant once more.

"Only family and friends have the house number?" Artemis clarified.

"That's what I said."

"Hey," Forester snapped. "Be polite to the lady."

Artemis gave a quick shake of her head. This didn't matter to her. She glanced up towards a window overlooking the driveway suddenly, spotting movement. A figure stood in the dark glass, like some sort of ghoul.

An older man, much older than Mrs. Watkins. He had an IV bag next to him and oxygen tubes attached to his face. His skin was pale, his head shaved. His fingers thin and bony, his arms wasting away. This was not a healthy man.

Artemis hesitated, then gave a small wave. The man in the window moved with ethereal motions and returned the gesture.

Mrs. Watkins frowned, stepped from the house and looked back. She sighed. "I told him to stay in bed. Carl!" she called, louder. "Carl go get some sleep! It's fine—just feds. The boys will be fine! Won't they?" she added, turning to look at Forester.

Forester just shrugged. "I mean... I don't really need much from them. You, Wade?"

"They attacked federal officers," Wade replied. "That's a *crime.*"

"Huh. True. But, you know, tough times and all that."

Wade let out a long, exasperated sigh. But Artemis was no longer listening. Pieces were slowly clicking into place. The man in the window, emaciated and small as he was, wouldn't have been able to drag metal lockers with trapped women through the forest or down concrete stairs. He didn't look like he could have uttered more than a sentence or two, much less entire conversations on the phone. And he certainly was in no shape to go stab his own mother in her home.

The Watkins in this house didn't look good for any of it. The two boys on the driveway were also too young to have been involved in decades-old murders.

But if Carl was as old as he looked... at least mid-sixties. Then what about his brother, Eli?

"So your brother-in-law," Artemis said, turning to Mrs. Watkins, "Was also cut out of the will?"

"Hmm?"

"Eli. He was cut out?"

"Oh. Yes. I think so."

"Wait, you *think* or you *know*?"

It took another long pause for Mrs. Watkins to register the question, but when it finally did, she sighed and said quietly, "I know that Isabel hated us. She hated my boys. She hated me. She missed the old days. Missed her husband. Missed her daughter."

"Desi?"

"Yes. But Isabel missed it all and took it out on us. She was a soulless shrew."

Artemis stiffened. "Soulless?"

161

"Hmm?"

"You called your mother-in-law soulless."

"Well, yes... perhaps a little harsh. But, unless you haven't noticed, things around here aren't easy. You might look at the horses and the flowers and the gardens. Envious sorts often do. But say one thing for money, it doesn't stop cancer. Still..." she trailed off, morose. "It would be nice to have some once Carl dies."

"What happens when your husband dies?" Artemis hesitated, winced and added quickly, "Not to be insensitive."

"It all goes up for sale. It's written in Isabel's will. It's sold at a public auction. None of us will see a cent."

"Not even Eli? Was he older or younger than Carl?"

"Older... A couple of years."

Artemis nodded slowly, her mind racing now. "And where is Eli Watkins?"

"Oh... probably out and about with that young friend of his."

"Which friend?"

"Jeb Arthur. Eli and Jeb are inseparable."

Artemis turned sharply. Wade was already typing something rapidly on his phone. "Does Eli have an address?" Artemis asked.

"Not really. He lives in an RV," she said. And there was a note of wistful regret in her voice. A distant look in her eyes to accompany it. The expression lingered enough for Artemis to wonder if there had been something of a history between Mrs. Watkins and her brother-in-law.

But Artemis ignored this train of thought.

Someone had called the house. Someone who had the number, and apparently the list of people who did was very exclusive. So exclusive that simply *having* the number warranted enough trust from the two knuckleheads to punch first and ask questions later.

But other things were now starting to make sense.

Why now? That was the question she had been asking herself.

Why had the killer chosen to start contacting the police now? Because of the inevitability of the bodies being discovered? He had waited until a jogger had stumbled on his pile of bones. But he had left Sierra with a tattoo of his number there, suggesting he had been expecting them. And not just expecting but wanting them to find her.

He could have just moved the bones. Tried to burn them. But no, he had wanted the bodies discovered. He had known they were there.

But why?

Artemis scowled, trying to piece it all together in her mind. Bits and pieces were starting to make sense. But one thing stood out. She knew why now.

The answer was in that upstairs room, behind the glass. A man dying of cancer. The sole recipient of his mother's estate and wealth. And when he died, a public auction.

Someone had chosen now as the perfect opportunity to start causing trouble. To start contacting the police and to shine a light on decades-old murders.

Artemis still had a niggling question in the back of her brain. She wanted to find the killer, not just for the sake of justice but also to find out about Helen.

The longer it took to locate this murderer, the longer she had to live with an unanswered question. Artemis had come back to the Misty North to find Helen, to confront her father.

But now, there was a chance that Helen had been kept, locked away like those women, and then killed later, perhaps buried in the woods with the rest.

Small, horrible thoughts, the sort of thoughts that left her with a weak feeling in her gut.

Either way, to answer the questions, she needed to find the killer.

And someone had chosen the misfortune of Carl Watkins as the perfect time to play hide and seek with the police. There was really only one suspect. The partner to Jeb Arthur—whom they had found sleeping in the barn next to the missing victim.

Artemis looked over at Agent Wade. "We need to find Eli Watkins."

"Already sent out an APB," he replied quickly. "I've got his driver's license here. The first name clears things up."

Artemis nodded but then glanced towards Mrs. Watkins. She hesitated, and, meeting the vacuous look in the woman's eyes, Artemis said, "Pardon me asking, but it's going to bother me if I don't; do you know why your mother-in-law was keeping old family photos locked in a box beneath her bed?"

It was the twins who answered this time. More accurately, the one twin who didn't seem to mind speaking. He grunted and said, "Because of the album thief."

"Excuse me?"

He looked ready to snap at her again but then shot a quick look towards Forester, cleared his throat, and in a reserved voice, said, "A couple of years ago, someone broke into the house and stole some photos. Apparently, they hit Nana's house too. After that, Nana—"

"Don't call her that!"

"Sorry, mom," he said, sheepishly, but then he continued. "She was paranoid that the thief would come back and try to take more pictures from her."

"Someone broke into both of your houses to steal pictures?"

"That's right."

"Did they take anything else?"

The twins as well as their mother all shook their heads. Artemis wrinkled her nose, puzzling at this strange clue. Why would someone break into a wealthy person's home just to steal photographs?

Either way, all roads seemed to point towards Eli Watkins.

Forester was busy uncuffing the two men, and Agent Wade was too distracted to protest. Forester reached into his pocket and pulled out a couple of business cards. Artemis rolled her eyes as she listened to the start of a familiar pitch. "If either of you two ever want to come down, we can teach you how to throw that overhand right."

Neither man accepted the cards. Forester tucked both slips of paper beneath the windshield wiper on the spaceship.

Agent Wade was mumbling something on his phone now, likely issuing further instructions for the APB.

For them to speak with Eli Watkins, they would first have to find him. And as Artemis considered it, she could think of at least one person, according to recent testimony, who might be able to locate the oldest Watkins brother.

Currently, though, the source of the information was in a jail cell, pending further investigation.

But it seemed like the best path forward.

To find Eli, they needed to speak with Jeb Arthur. They needed him to admit how he'd been involved in all of this.

CHAPTER 18

Jeb Arthur wasn't nearly as recalcitrant this time. Artemis sat in the cold, metal seat across the table now, next to Agent Wade.

Forester leaned against the glass behind Jeb's seat, forcing the man to twist his head if he wanted to keep an eye on the agent.

Wade frowned at Jeb. "We know you were involved, Mr. Arthur. We know Eli Watkins is the killer."

Jeb didn't blink. He just paused, then snorted beneath his breath, shaking his head side to side. "Who told you that shit?"

Wade shot back. "Carl Watkins' family implied it."

"Carl is dying. He didn't say that."

"His wife, then," Wade said. "*Heavily* implied it."

Jeb shook his head. "Nah."

"Yes," said Wade.

"Nah," Jeb repeated.

Artemis studied the man's expression. She didn't speak at first, preferring to watch her opponent across the table. Sweat on his forehead. His easy manner, his would-be indifference, was a tell. Yesterday, he'd been all bluster and brash. Today, though?

Calmer. Easy-going. Snide and indifferent.

She could think of a few things that led to a drastic person-ality shift, but one of them—no doubt—was fear.

"Tell me about Eli Watkins," Artemis said quietly.

Jeb shook his head. "Nothing to tell."

"Why was he cut out of his mother's will?"

"Didn't know that happened."

"You're lying," Artemis said. She didn't blink. "I can tell. The rest of it, not sure yet. But that part was a lie."

He shifted uncomfortably now. Of course, Artemis didn't *know* anything. But oftentimes, her father had said that the best way to throw someone off their game was to convince them that *other* powers were at play.

A guess could do that. A guess she *missed* would be forgot-ten, allowing her to try again later.

But a guess she hit?

Questions would start whirring through a subject's mind. *How did she know that? Who has she been talking to?*

It was little more than a trick that most parents played with their prepubescent children. Sitting them down across the table, asking them if there was anything they needed to know, then making a guess... without evidence... to stir the pot.

Did you finish your homework? You didn't clean your room how I asked, did you?

Any number of small questions, followed by a guess. It all came back to putting someone on their back foot. Disturbing their sense of confidence in their ability to hide the unknown.

And now, judging by his reaction, she'd been right.

He *did* know that Eli had been cut out of his mother's will. Only a small tidbit. But this was the open door she would pry on. His mind would already be working against him. *Who is this woman? How did she know that? What else does she know? Who has she been talking to?*

Artemis leaned forward now, studying Mr. Arthur, refusing to blink. "You *know* why Eli was cut out of the will, don't you?" Repeating already established information, creating a base upon which to launch a second salvo. Double guessing—a dangerous game. But women were dying. So Artemis went for it. "In fact, you knew that Eli was furious about it, didn't you?"

A miss. His face relaxed. He leaned back a bit.

This was the risk of the double-guess. Now she'd have to restart. Looking at his expression, she felt confident Eli *hadn't* been angry about being removed from the will. That didn't make sense, did it?

Now it was her turn to adopt a poker face and to keep her expression casual. Back at square one.

This was the risk of overplaying her hand. Neither agent, watching her, even realized what she was fishing for. Perhaps didn't know that she *was* fishing. But the preamble to a match was often as important as the match itself. Most of her opponents in the realm of chess were equally susceptible to insinuation.

As she studied the man, she considered a follow-up question, pivoting tactically. Square one didn't mean she had nothing to work with. Rapid fire was also a way to disorient.

And so she shot the next question, "You know *why* he was left out of the will, don't you?"

Bingo.

She struck gold on that one.

His eyes told the story. A faint, nervous glance to the side; he rubbed at his wrist. He looked up again and his chair scraped the ground as he readjusted.

Artemis studied him closely, then nodded. "Why was Eli Watkins cut from his mother's will?"

"I don't know."

"You do."

"I don't!"

"You're lying!"

"Bitch—ow!" He'd tried to lunge from his seat, but a combination of his handcuffs and Forester grabbing him and yanking sent him back into his chair.

Artemis flinched but recovered and kept her eyes on Mr. Arthur. "There's no point in lying," she said quietly. "Why save him? Mr. Arthur, save yourself. Were you involved in the murders?"

"Course he was involved," Forester muttered.

Artemis nodded at the man. "See, Jeb? Even the feds think you're in on it. Do they have the death penalty around these parts, Forester?"

"Hmm, might have to look into that. What do you think, Jeb?"

Mr. Arthur was shaking now, the blood having left his face. He shook his head rapidly from side to side, paused, stuttered, then slumped. Gone was the belligerence, gone was the anger.

But that left the question of why...

Why was Mr. Arthur so deflated all of a sudden? Because they'd mentioned the name of his friend. Eli Watkins was over sixty. Jeb Arthur couldn't have been much past his late thirties. Artemis knew of killers in their early teens. It was possible Jeb had been the one behind the mass burial scenes.

But also possible they'd been a team.

"Was that it?" Artemis said slowly. "The two of you? Both involved, hmm? Which of you would kidnap your victims? Whose idea was the metal lockers? We still don't know what your weapon was—care to share? Some knife? Something else."

"I didn't kill anyone!" he said, his voice shaking.

Artemis scowled back at him. "Yeah right!"

"I didn't! I wasn't..." he swallowed. "I wasn't at the barn to... to *hurt* anyone!" He looked up, eyes panicked. And for a flicker of a moment, Artemis paused. He looked... like he was telling the truth.

She frowned now. How could that be, though? He must have known about the woman in the basement. He had been only a hundred feet away in the barn. He'd been the caretaker of the ranch. He'd been involved on Watkins land, near the burial sites. His *own phone* number, listed from two years ago then discontinued, had been the number tattooed on Sierra, the number the killer had used.

So why did he look panicked now? Why did he look upset?

Jeb Arthur met her gaze, opened his mouth, paused, bit his lip, and went quiet again.

She stared at him a moment longer. Then, slowly, she said, "How did Desi Watkins die? The sister?"

"Umm—what?"

"How did Desi die?" Artemis murmured. "Surely that's something you can tell me."

"She went missing."

"How old?"

"Late teens. Don't remember much about it."

Artemis paused, desperately trying not to think of her own sister. Desi, Carl and Eli were a generation older, though. She paused, considering her next question, then said, quiet as a church mouse, "I bet Eli didn't care at all about her death, did he?"

Jeb's eyes suddenly flared with rage. Some of the anger from before erupted as he yelled, "How dare you! Eli was brokenhearted! He still thinks about his sister to this day!"

Artemis leaned back, nodding slowly. "That's what I thought," she said. Her skin buzzed; she watched Jeb closely.

Forester and Wade were both waiting then glancing at her, hesitant as if waiting for some follow-up. Artemis tapped her fingers against her leg, drumming them in a rolling pattern. She tried to inhale, to exhale slowly. She wanted to piece it all together, and this outburst... the *timing* of this outburst was another puzzle piece.

But in order to build a puzzle, one was often advised to start with the corners. The *known* quantities.

She raised a finger, pressing it against the table until the tip whitened. Then, quietly, she said, "Eli was brokenhearted... he still thinks about his missing sister to this day." She looked up, her own eyes sad as she met Jeb Arthur's glare. "You got angry when I said Eli didn't care. Why *that* angry? Over an employer? A friend? A close friend, yes? A very strange pairing, you two. Eli is what, thirty years your senior?"

"Twe—umm, I don't know." Jeb looked panicked now, frozen in his seat.

Artemis sighed, nodding slowly. "I see," she murmured. "You and Eli weren't friends, were you? That's why he was written out of his mother's will. The Watkins family—a pillar of the community, right?"

"The old hag was living in the past," Jeb Arthur snapped. "Soulless bitch!"

Artemis blinked. The second time someone had used the term *soulless.* The same term the killer had used.

And yet... "You and Eli were lovers."

"Go to hell."

"It's not an accusation," Artemis said quietly, her voice soft now. She could see the pain in the man's eyes. The rejection. Could see years of baggage. "That's why you said Eli didn't care he was written out of the will."

"I said go to hell."

"Watch it," Forester snapped.

"No, it's fine," Artemis said quickly.

But Jeb jutted his chin at her. "Oh, fine? Now you stand up for me against this big goon? What—cuz you think I'm delicate now? Think I need your protection? I've been protecting myself just fine. For years! You don't know what you're talking about!"

Artemis weathered the storm of words without blinking. Once he finished, she said slowly, "I'm not standing up for you because I think you're... *delicate.* But because I think you're innocent."

"Wait, what?" Forester said, frowning over the man's shoulder.

Wade just watched the exchange quietly, his eyes hooded.

Artemis nodded slowly, her heart weary. "Eli Watkins used you," she said faintly. "That's why you were at the barn. Let me guess; he made a call. Asked you to meet him there?"

She pictured the scene now. The bedding on the hay. Jeb Arthur with his finger on the trigger. But as she pictured the scene in her mind, she noticed something else. She closed her eyes, focusing on the image for a moment. Then, softly, she said, "Forester..."

"Checkers, about the whole innocence—"

"Give me a moment, please. The thing on the side of a gun... the little niggly thing."

"The trigger?"

Her eyes were still closed as she shook her head. "No... No, not that. The other thing."

"The... sights?"

"No, the thing on the side. Near the thumb."

"Oh, the safety?"

"Yes." She opened her eyes again. "Jeb Arthur's safety was on the entire time, in the standoff. It wasn't until you lunged that he flicked it. He did it fast."

Forester frowned. "Doesn't mean he didn't kill those women."

But Artemis watched Mr. Arthur. "Did Eli call you? Ask you to rendezvous? Maybe like old times?" As she said it, she felt a flicker of unease, remembering her own text messages with Jamie.

Forester looked uncomfortable with this line of questioning, massaging his calloused knuckles against the inside of his off-hand. Forester frowned, shaking his head. "You're saying Eli Watkins is the killer?"

"He isn't!" Jeb yelled.

Wade's phone began to ring, and the agent stood up, answering it.

Forester snorted at Mr. Arthur. "I'm not buying it. You wanted some of that money from the will, didn't you? So you and Eli planned to kill the old lady. You also killed all those other women. Didn't you?"

"No!"

"Tell the truth!"

"I am!" Jeb was yelling again, his temper getting the better of him. Up to this point, Artemis noticed he hadn't directly contradicted her inference.

But now, she was shaking her head, trying to piece the information together from this *new* angle.

If Jeb Arthur had been used by Eli Watkins, unknowingly even, then that meant, perhaps, he'd been an unwitting accomplice to murder.

"You brought up my phone number, before!" Jeb said suddenly. "Eli doesn't have it! It was stolen from me two years ago!"

"Wait, stolen?" Artemis asked.

"Yes—the phone had a sim card. Old type. The number was taken when the phone was."

"Eli Watkins must have taken your phone," Forester said.

"He didn't—I *know* he didn't!"

Artemis felt her heart break at the pain in Mr. Arthur's voice. But she also couldn't let compassion blind her. Just because she could now explain *why* Jeb was defending Eli, didn't mean he wasn't still somehow involved.

Her instincts suggested he wasn't. The safety on the gun. The absolute surprise. The look in his eyes...

But that didn't *mean* he wasn't playing her.

Even a pulse, or tears, or a posture could be manipulated.

Forester was still glaring at the back of Jeb's head. Clearly, he wasn't buying the man's innocence. Mr. Arthur was still protesting. Artemis was trying to complete the puzzle.

But it came crashing down when Wade spoke.

"They found him," Wade said.

Artemis glanced over. Forester looked up in excitement.

Jeb said, "Eli? Where is he? He didn't do this!"

But Wade cut the man off, his expression grim. "They found him in his RV. Parked at a long-term camping spot—the owner recognized the plate from a news bulletin."

"And?" Artemis said, already feeling a slow sense of dread as she read Wade's tone.

"And," the agent said with a sigh, "He's been dead for at least a week. Whole place stinks. Corpse was half eaten by some critter that came in the window. Eli Watkins is dead."

Jeb Arthur went as still as a ghost. His eyes widening. For a moment, Artemis watched as tears brimmed. Watched as the man began to hyperventilate.

Then Forester said, "Really? Where?"

"Wade, Forester," Artemis cut in, teeth set. "If you don't mind?" She nodded towards the door. Then shot a quick glance towards Arthur.

She realized a second later, though, Wade was also watching him shrewdly.

Jeb was breathing rapidly, blinking and refusing to look up as he stared at a faint reflection in the metal of the table.

Wade watched the man a moment longer, then seemed to reach a decision. His normally stoic features arranged into an apologetic wince. "Sorry, pal." Then he turned, pushing through the door. Artemis and Forester followed quickly into the hall.

CHAPTER 19

"What the hell was that?" Artemis said, irritated. "Why are you discussing his friend's death in front of him like that?"

Wade sighed, nodding. "I know. That was ugly. I wanted to make sure he didn't know."

Forester snorted, leaning back against the metal of the interrogation room door. A vending machine down the hall glowed and buzzed with a bluish light. "He's faking," Forester said. "I'd bet anything."

"How about half of your ego?" Artemis snapped. "I think you'd lose."

Forester raised an eyebrow. "What's got you all worked up?"

She paused, considering it. Then she slumped against the wall as well. She had to remember these two men were FBI agents. Had been for years. Jaded to the job.

For her, though, sitting in a room like that, watching an angry man choose rage instead of pain... it... hurt.

She was used to hating the man across the table. Hating people like her father and everything they stood for.

But someone like Jeb Arthur? He'd been used. A pawn...

But no. No, that didn't make sense anymore. If Eli Watkins was *dead.*

"They're sure it was Eli?" Artemis asked.

"Only the bottom half was eaten," Wade said conversationally. "They think it was some bobcat. Head was identified. It's Eli."

"Then..." Artemis trailed off, shaking her head. "He can't be our killer."

"Nope," said Forester. He jammed a thumb over his shoulder. "Because our killer is sitting in there. I know you've got a soft spot for sob stories, Checkers, but he's playing you hard. I checked out that blog you mentioned. The one with the old news clippings—did you know Jeb Arthur's family has been on Watkins land for generations? They're in it together, Artemis."

"The blog didn't say that."

"No, but the clues are there if you're willing to look."

She glared at Forester, pointing towards the metal door. "You know, there's a fine line between cavalier and cruel."

Forester leaned forward now, standing a foot away—which only served to emphasize his height. He looked down at her, his brow crinkled. His untamed hair frazzled in the buzzing blue light from the vending machine.

"The job isn't pretty, Ms. Blythe. It isn't *nice.* Cavalier and cruel is sometimes all there is. You want to talk about a suspect's feelings? Go be a damn therapist!"

She glared right back at him. "Not everyone lacks a heart, Cameron!"

He shrugged. "Maybe you should try it, doll. Might help you see a bit clearer. That guy," Forester jammed a finger towards the door, "is a liar. I can smell it a mile away. He's involved. I guarantee it."

"And I say he isn't!"

Wade sighed, slumping against the vending machine and leaning back until his close, military-cut hair glowed blue. "You two done?"

"No!" Forester and Artemis snapped at the same time. They returned their glares to each other.

Artemis wanted to lash out. She was tired, cranky, lacking both sleep and sustenance.

Part of her was terrified that she was wrong. Forester had a point. The agent had been investigating crimes far longer than she had. If he said Arthur was involved, then maybe she was deluding herself.

But another, more instinctual part of her refused to concede the point. Granted, she hadn't been the one nearly shot by Jeb Arthur. Perhaps that was clouding Forester's vision. On the other hand, that same instinctual sense suggested that she was clearly missing something.

She turned away from Forester, refusing to stare down the fighter. She wondered how many times he had faced off from an opponent like that, only a day or two before pummeling them in a cage.

She shook her head, trying not to think too harshly of Cameron. It wasn't his fault that he had been born with an abnormal emotional makeup. She knew that he was no stranger to loss. Glimpses, murmurs, things she had seen and heard told her that Forester knew pain.

Cavalier and cruel were two very good ways of preventing one's self from experiencing more pain.

She shook her head, trying not to distract herself. "If Eli is dead," she said quietly, "then it means he couldn't have killed his mother. He couldn't have been on the phone with me. And he couldn't have been the one who kidnapped those two women."

Wade nodded, pointing at her as if keeping track of some score.

Forester shot back, "Which means, the only suspect we have is sitting in *that* room. He might have a sob story, but that doesn't mean he isn't a killer. He would have been young, a teen at best, for his first kills. But I've heard of younger doing worse. He was on the farm; his phone number called you—it's him."

"And his *current* number—which you have in evidence, doesn't match. *Plus*, he was in jail. He couldn't have killed Isabel," Artemis snapped back.

"He hired someone," Forester retorted.

"You don't actually think that. What's up with you? Why are you so confident this guy is the killer?"

"Because..." Forester said, slowly, enunciating his words. "He's the best suspect! The evidence points to *him*. The real question is why don't you?"

Artemis paused; she considered this, and then realized if she gave an honest response it would likely only elicit mockery. Her *instincts* weren't evidence. Though the agents had been willing to go along with them in the past.

But also, the safety on the shotgun. A small, *very* small, detail. But Arthur's shotgun had only been fired *after* Forester had lunged, physically threatening him. Keeping the safety on wasn't the behavior of a killer.

Plus... what was it he'd said... someone had stolen his old phone with the number the killer had used?

Someone had also been stealing photo albums from the Watkins families. That was why Isabel had hidden her photos under her bed in a locked box.

So what did it mean?

Artemis let out a long sigh, closing her eyes. She turned and shook her head. "I need to get some sleep."

Wade cleared his throat. "You don't want to come see the RV crime scene?"

"He's been dead a week?" she called over her shoulder.

"Preliminary report. But yeah."

"Then no," she replied. "Take pictures if you want. But no. If Eli isn't our killer and if Jeb isn't, then the real monster is still out there."

To Forester's credit, he held his tongue this time.

But she wasn't exactly in the credit-giving mood. She marched past the buzzing, blue vending machine. And as she moved towards the sliding doors of the precinct, her head slumped and she felt the weight of the world descend on her shoulders.

CHAPTER 20

Rain. The one thing Washington could always offer to make a bad situation worse. She slipped from the front seat of the taxi, biting her lip. Wondering if she was making a mistake.

She moved under the dim evening sky, taking hurried steps towards the small shelter in the equally small park. She recognized the park. She'd often visited it back in her younger years.

But now, as she hurried forward, she wondered if she ought to just retreat.

But he'd called, hadn't he?

He'd *wanted* to meet.

And she... she wanted to meet as well.

As she hastened away from the parked taxi, waving quickly in gratitude, she half hunched her head and shoulders. Not that it helped against the rain in the least.

If anything, it only gave the rain somewhere to pool along her neck and shoulders. But as the water speckled her head, her skin, her arms, she moved quickly under the cover of the red, wooden gazebo on the edge of the park. The lake vibrated as droplets tap-danced across the surface.

She listened to the hum of the water. She shivered as droplets fell from her skin. She raised her phone.

Running a couple behind. Can't wait to see you!

She smiled. Jamie Kramer was on his way.

She leaned back against a wooden rail, listening to the downpour and studying her phone. Perhaps she should have gone with the agents to investigate the newest crime scene.

But even as she thought it, her stomach did a flip, rebelling against the notion.

Forester was behaving like an ass...

Or maybe...

Maybe Forester was just behaving like himself. And it was only now getting to her. She frowned at the thought. Her respect towards Agent Wade grew. The man had put up with being Forester's partner far longer than Artemis had been forced to work with the man.

But another part of her had to admit the truth.

Forester wasn't *wrong.* Jeb Arthur *was* their best suspect. She just didn't believe he was the right one. But what frustrated her most was that she didn't know where else to look for a *better* suspect. Rain tapped around her, pooling on the roof of the gazebo, then falling in sheets.

She shifted from foot to foot, her fingers drumming against the damp wooden railing now. She glanced at her phone again, then her eyes found the parking lot.

Exhaustion weighed, as did her conscience. Was she making some horrible mistake? Artemis felt too tired now. Another part of her felt like a stone, skimming across the surface of the lake. If ever she lost forward momentum, she would sink.

She stared at the pond, frowning, wondering what was hidden beneath the surface. She didn't want to admit the truth. But a part of her wondered if she would ever find out what really happened to Helen?

The most likely option: her father had killed his daughter. But...

But what if...

Artemis shook her head. The coroner's report had come in slowly, as victims were identified. So far, Helen hadn't been found among the dead.

Which meant what?

Artemis scowled, leaning back now. Her phone buzzed again.

She glanced down, expecting a text from Jamie. Her heart skipped, partly in anticipation, and partly in dread, wondering if he'd decided to cancel their meet-up last minute.

What she found, however, was entirely unexpected.

A number she didn't recognize. She wrinkled her nose. For a horrible moment, she thought perhaps the killer was contacting her again.

But no...

No, the words weren't goading or mocking. They were words of concern. Of placation.

Artemis re-read them twice.

Thanks...don't wory abou me. I'me fine. Bye.

The spelling errors aside, which helped Artemis rule out the "Professor" as the sender of the message, Artemis noticed how polite the message was. Gratitude. And a farewell.

Who is this? She texted back.

Briefly, she felt confident she wouldn't hear back. So it was with some surprise that the number responded. *That place was too scarey. So I left. Thanks. Bye.*

Artemis' eyes widened in realization. "No way..." she murmured. She tried calling the number but was instantly sent to voicemail. She tried texting again. *Where are you?*

But this time, no response.

Artemis leaned back, staring at her phone. She wasn't sure how to feel at first. Was it really the woman from the ranch basement? She was alive! She was well!

Artemis let out a long breath, realizing just how much pent-up guilt she'd been harboring.

She bit her lip nervously, though. What if it was a trick? What if the killer was playing games with her?

But the earnestness of the messages, the spelling errors... hinted at some type of authenticity. Didn't it? Unless that was what the killer wanted her to think. It was the sort of message a man like her father might send in order to deceive.

Artemis tried calling the number again, but again it went straight to a voicemail box that hadn't been set up yet.

She sighed, re-reading the message again and feeling at least some small amount of relief. The not *knowing* was the hardest part.

"Hey!"

She nearly dropped her phone, turning sharply. A man was hastening towards her through the rain, a large, puffy sweater turning damp under the deluge. He reached the shelter in the park a few seconds later, his damp shoes leaving dark stains on the gray floor as water soaked into the cement.

And then, shaking his head, dislodging more droplets, Jamie Kramer's sea-gray eyes found hers.

Artemis' phone dropped into her pocket now. She realized her fingers were trembling and she quickly smoothed the front of her shirt in order to still her hand. "Hey," she replied, giving a quick smile.

Jamie stood a few paces away, lingering in the entrance to the gazebo where he watched her. Silence hung between them now. It had been... too long since they'd last spoken. The last couple of times had been by phone. By text.

In person, though, the last time had followed a tragedy.

She could pick out the damage in Jamie's posture. In his eyes. Pain always left a mark, and over a lifetime of experiencing it, Artemis had learned to recognize it in others. A normally easy smile was absent from Jamie's lips. She remembered those lips well.

His sea-gray eyes weren't the calm, tranquil waters she remembered. There were waves in those eyes. An agitation that went deep. Bags under the eyes hinted at exhaustion. He was now taking care of his baby sister who'd also been orphaned.

"How's Sophie?" Artemis blurted out, then she bit her lip, wondering if she ought to have said something different.

But Jamie just flashed a tired smile. "Fine... fine. Figuring out routines still, you know. I've never been... well... a dad before." He shook his head. "Not that... well, not that I am. Definitely not a good one. I'm still big brother Jamie." He said this last part with another shake of his head.

"She listens to you, though?"

"Yeah, Sophie's a good kid. I mean... after everything, I'm not sure it's really sunk in yet..." He trailed off, running a hand through the fringe of his hair.

She watched Jamie where he stood, his form outlined against the gray skies and steady deluge. He was paler than the last time she'd seen him, his dark eyes set in a faint, olive complexion. His square jaw was more *masculine* than *neanderthal* and his features were arranged on the pretty side of manly, with long eyelashes and high cheekbones.

But the thing she had always liked most about Jamie was his warmth.

In a place as cold as Pinelake and the surrounding towns, Jamie was a hearth fire. Even standing there, his sea-gray eyes flickering from the water-dappled floor back up to her, she was taken in again by those eyes. Eyes that had always held a sort of concern, of compassion.

For a moment, she felt as if she was a teenager again.

One of the last times they'd spoken in person, though, Jamie Kramer had lied to her. This was a rarity for the man. Honest, eventually.

That's how she'd seen him. Honest.

Eventually.

But he'd said that he'd interviewed with the sheriff of Pinelake for a salesman position. But the sheriff had contradicted this point. A five-and-a-half hour interview from what Artemis remembered. But she still didn't know what for.

It wasn't important. Didn't seem vital compared to everything else that had happened.

But one thing Artemis Blythe couldn't abide was a liar.

"Why did you meet with Sheriff Dawkins all those weeks ago?" she said simply.

He looked up again. Their gaze lingered on each other. He scratched his chin, glanced off, shrugged. "Umm..." He massaged the bridge of his nose. "Honestly, seems silly now."

"Was it a salesman position?" she said, innocently.

He snorted. "You always do that."

"Do what?"

"Set traps with your words," he said. It wasn't a harsh rebuke. His eyes were still gentle, but there was a note of bitterness to his voice.

"So it wasn't?"

"No, Artemis," he said with a long breath. "It wasn't for a salesman position. The sheriff wants me to run for mayor. At least, he *did*. He felt my family's connections, wealth—roots in the community—would give us a good shot at victory. Plus, well... he seemed to think he could control me."

Honest. Eventually.

Jamie ran a hand through his wet hair, lowering his palm and rubbing it off on his shirt. "I guess that ship has sailed. Ever since... well, mom and dad." Another bitter note. "The sheriff hasn't been nearly so keen."

"I'm sorry."

"For what?"

"For asking."

"Don't be sorry for asking. I shouldn't have lied to you."

"Jamie Kramer, mayor." Artemis gave a little smile. "It has a nice ring to it."

"Not anymore," Jamie said, a sad look in his gaze. "Not after what dad did. After what happened to mom." He shook his head. "Sorry. We don't have to talk about that."

"Umm. No... It's... it's fine." Artemis glanced off at the pond again, watching the way the rain disturbed the water. She wanted to meet Jamie's gaze. Wanted to hold it. But at the mention of his parents, she felt her heart sink.

She had been present when his father had been shot. In fact, his father had been trying to kill her. The Ghost-killer had sent him, according to Mr. Kramer. Her own father had his hand in everything, manipulating people like puppets.

Now, she couldn't meet Jamie's gaze.

But he cleared his throat, and, drawing her attention, he said, "Did you see him die?"

A dreadful question. One she had hoped to never answer. Especially not to Jamie. "Do you really want me to tell you?" She said, biting her lip.

"Yes."

"I was there."

"Did you kill him?" There was no emotion in his voice. When she didn't reply right away, he quickly added, "I wouldn't blame you. I know he was sick. I didn't know *how* sick. After what he did to mom, to those other women..." Jamie's face twisted, and a flash of rage crossed his expression. After another trailing moment, in which Artemis allowed the question to sit, he said, "How do you do it?"

"Do what?"

"Live with it? Knowing what your dad did? Knowing how wrong you were about him? God, you were only a kid. I was a grown-ass man. I didn't see it. I was angry at my mother. I took my father's side. I gave him my damn ring."

"Jamie, stop it," she said. She was surprised by how harsh her voice was.

He looked up in surprise.

"It's not your fault," she said simply. "You don't have the luxury to throw a pity party. Sophie needs you. Trust me. I have a brother too. He's been living in the past more than he has any right to. He thinks because dad hurt him, he's allowed to do whatever the hell he wants."

"That's not what I'm saying."

"I-I know. I'm sorry. I... You have every right to be angry." She grimaced, feeling sad all of a sudden. Then, in a timid voice, she murmured, "What *are* you saying?"

He rubbed at his face, shaking his head. "Honestly, I don't know."

They trailed off again, and the sounds of their voices were replaced by the drumming rain.

Artemis took a step towards him but hesitated. He looked so sad standing there, damp, wearing a baggy sweater instead of the banker suit like last time.

She wanted to hug him. Wanted to wrap her arms around his warm form and tell him everything was going to be okay. Another, smaller, far more childish part of her wanted to grab his hand and run off into the woods. Onto those same mountain slopes where they had shared their first kiss. She wanted to know what those lips still tasted like. Wanted to know if they were as soft as she remembered. If he would stroke her hair and whisper things in her ear.

The moonlight reminded her of Jamie Kramer. The scent of moss, of the forest, of even the rain. She could remember the times they snuck out of the large mansion, moving up the trail into the woods. Often, Tommy would join them. And though she liked the time spent with her brother well enough, her favorite times had been with Jamie alone.

And so, she wanted to hold him, to run away, to find freedom in the forest again.

But what about Sophie? What about the killer targeting these women?

What about Helen? And what about the Ghost-killer and whatever he had in store for the town?

People were well-versed in their freedom and the rights they had. Very few considered the responsibilities they owed others.

Responsibilities weren't things to mandate, weren't a thing to bludgeon someone with. If done this way, they would be shirked, neglected and resented. True responsibility, always directed towards someone else, for their benefit, was a thing to choose.

She couldn't run off into the woods with Jamie.

"Do you hate me?" she said. She didn't realize where the question had even come from. Her voice sounded faint and childish to her own ears.

As she said it, though, Jamie looked up, surprised. "Hate you? Why would I hate you?"

"Because I couldn't help him. Because I was there when he died."

"He deserved to die, Artemis. He was a murderer. I don't hate you. I understand you more than ever." Those gray eyes flashed. "You were only fifteen," he said, his voice shaking. "And you turned out, well, perfect."

"I'm not perfect. Not even close."

"I'm an adult, and what he did is tearing me apart. Some days," Jamie said, in a whisper of a voice, as if he didn't want the world to hear too much, "when I wake up, and I think about it all, about my life, about what I have to do, I just want to..." He trailed off, a look of shame in his gaze. He swallowed. He gave a quick shake of his head. "I'm sorry, I don't mean to bore you." He forced a smile.

But she reached out, hesitantly, her thumb grazing his cheek. She found the edge of his lips and tugged, insistently. He allowed her to manipulate his expression until the smile vanished.

Honest, eventually.

Her hand lingered against his face. She didn't want to lift it. She didn't want much to change. Standing there, in the gazebo, in the park, against the pond, with rain drumming around them, it almost felt like the woods. It almost felt like those stolen nights at fifteen.

She leaned in suddenly, unsure what she was doing.

Her hand rested against his chest. The cold of the rain competed with the warmth of his body. She looked up, studying his lips. Then her eyes closed, briefly. She leaned in, also briefly.

But there wasn't much brief about the moment that followed.

Her lips found his. He didn't recoil. She leaned against him, her body pressed to his. His hand found the small of her back, cradling her, holding her close and near. He breathed softly as he withdrew, tentative. The warmth of his breath pressed to her cheeks.

Artemis lingered back, only an inch away, hovering. Her eyes still closed, the sensation spreading from her lips. Her skin now buzzed. Her face too. Her cheeks prickled.

Excitement hammered in her chest. But also other thoughts. She was thirty years old, but she felt like a child. She thought silly things. Wondering if her hair was too damp. Wondering if she'd done it wrong. Wondering if she'd pressed too hard. Dear God, had she pursed her lips like someone sucking a lemon? And her chest—she'd never had a very

191

large chest. Dammit—she'd leaned against him. He must have felt how small her chest was. And what about the way she'd cocked her leg, leaning forward? What did she think she was? Some Disney princess?

The thoughts cycled in rapid accusation. A moment that had started as pure instinct turned to one of true criticism. She even felt a knot forming in her stomach, spreading. Felt her heart beginning to pound. Fanciful, silly thoughts had prompted her to kiss Jamie Kramer.

But now, her analytical mind returned. And she found herself so sorely lacking.

He whispered something though.

Those two words caught her attention. She hesitated, eyes flickering open, studying his mouth.

"You're perfect..." he said.

"I'm not," she replied.

"I don't care."

He kissed her this time. More firmly. He held her now, his hand moving to cradle her head, her shoulders. She leaned back a bit as he pressed towards her, as if intent on becoming one. As if introducing his soul to hers.

Jamie's lips were as soft as she remembered. Her skin prickled as she remembered.

In fact, standing there, leaning back, caught in an embrace, it didn't feel as if the trees or the woods or the secret trips to the mountains were that important after all.

The two separated, if only to breathe. And even then, with some reluctance.

They both stood, exhaling heavily, staring at each other, then looking away bashfully, but shooting sidelong glances back. Jamie Kramer could have had any girl in school. Now, he could have had any girl in town.

And yet... he was acting like a schoolboy, too. It was probably her effect. She was causing his discomfort. She shifted again, uncomfortable all of a sudden.

Jamie flinched. "Did—did I hurt you?"

"No!" she said. Too loud. Too damn loud.

"Oh. Good." He looked crestfallen.

"You didn't!" she insisted.

"Oh. I mean... You just... you look upset."

"What? No—no, not... not at you!"

"At who?"

"Me. I'm... I'm not a very good kisser. I tried. I... I'm sorry, I didn't even mean to do that." She rambled now, prattling, shaking her head, wishing she wasn't talking so much then wishing she could figure out a way to stop.

Jamie stared. "You're... you're the best kisser I've ever met! I mean... with you... It matters. It... it's different." He blushed now. "Not that I've kissed very many people."

"I've only kissed one." The moment she said it, she wished she hadn't. She wondered how pathetic it must have sounded to him. This whole business bothered her. Standing there, awkward and shy. She missed the precision of a match. Missed tactical engagement, deep analysis, preparation. She knew those things.

This...

Whatever *this* was...

Terrified her. Made her feel small. She wasn't Artemis Blythe, genius chess master, in this moment. She was little Artemis, awkward and shy.

Jamie came close again, but this time his arms wrapped around her. He held her, and she felt the little accusations melt away again. The icy cocoon thawing in the warmth of her childhood sweetheart. "You know," she murmured. "You're perfect too."

"I'm not," he replied.

"Good," she said, her voice a murmur. She nestled against his chest, inhaling and exhaling and listening as he did the same, absorbing his warmth in such a cold place. The shelter above, the only thing protecting them from the downpour.

She could have stayed there for hours. She wanted to.

Jamie was murmuring now, whispering. "I got the gold... I... I invested in some land. A hundred acres. Did I already tell you? We're building a house. It's only an hour from here."

"That sounds nice," Artemis whispered. She couldn't remember whether he'd mentioned this before or not. She couldn't remember much of anything.

He chuckled. "I might become a rancher. Get some horses."

"I saw horses today," she said, still absentmindedly.

As she spoke, though, her brow furrowed. The thought of the Watkins' farm cast her back into colder waters, darker thoughts.

And though she leaned against a source of warmth, her mind braved the cold. It was dragged away, unbidden, against its will.

Artemis' frown was now curdling the cloth on Jamie's shoulder. She tried to return to the warmth, but another part of her was spinning again.

Over thirty years the killer had buried his victims on the Watkins' mountain. He'd known about mineshafts of secret gold-mining operations from a hundred years ago.

He'd led the police to the Wishing Well property with his clues. Effectively sending search parties traipsing over the private land for days. Why would he do that?

What was his game?

And why start playing with the police *now* of all things? Carl was dying. Why did that matter?

As for his interest in her... creepy as it was, it was a separate issue. But it suggested something.

The killer was local. The buried corpses suggested the same thing, of course.

And then, suddenly, Artemis looked up. "Public auction," she murmured.

Jamie glanced down, leaning back. "Hmm?"

"How did you buy that land? A hundred acres, you said?"

"Just found it online, I suppose."

"It wasn't an auction?"

"Not really big enough to be auctioned. Why?"

Artemis disentangled from Jamie now, turning towards the rain and pacing in the small gazebo. She frowned as she did. "That's what Mrs. Watkins said. Once her husband died, the land would be sent to public auction. Isabel Watkins is dead. Which means her will is enacted. So everything goes to Carl. But Carl has cancer; he'll be gone soon. And then?"

"Then? What are you talking about, Artemis?"

"I'm... I'm working with the FBI again."

"Oh?"

"Mhmm." She tried to give a reassuring nod, but her mind was distant, still considering every angle. The warm kiss seemed a distant memory now.

And suddenly, it struck her.

The land.

"Someone's driving down the price of the land," she said simply. She looked at Jamie. "That's the key. The land. The mountain with the bodies."

"Wait, *bodies*?"

"Oh, yes. Sorry." She winced apologetically then resumed her pacing, her fingers finding her phone now and pulling it from her pocket. She twisted it in her hand, allowing it to spin, spin, spin. It's the only reason the killer is coming forward now.

Carl is dying. He knew he was going to kill Isabel. Eli was written out of the will. No one else gets anything. The land goes to public auction. So he's driving down the price. He wanted the bodies found. Wanted the story in the news. Wanted police to search those mountains, crawling up and down. He wanted helicopters flying overhead. He wanted the FBI involved, traipsing over the Wishing Well. He wanted Jeb Arthur arrested—which is why he placed the call from the old number, luring Jeb to the same spot. It's why he killed Eli!"

Artemis' heart was racing now.

"I'm... I'm afraid I don't know..." Jamie paused. "Would you like me to just stand here quietly and listen?"

"Mhmm."

"Done. Please proceed."

Artemis flashed a quick smile but continued her pacing. "What I don't understand," she said, "is why go to such measures to tarnish the name of the Watkins family? To run down the price of their land? He wants the land, clearly, but *why*?"

"Umm... Well... I mean, land around here is actually supposed to start dropping in price. I don't think it's due to increase for a bit."

Artemis frowned. "So there's no money in the land?"

"I mean... Not *much.* Property taxes alone are killer."

"And there's no gold in the mountains... It's empty."

"So?"

"So..." Artemis said slowly. "Why does he want to buy the land so badly?"

"If it's a public auction, maybe you can wait and see who bids..."

"It's a good point," she said, "But that won't be until Carl Watkins dies. He's not doing well, but he's still around."

"I see."

Artemis frowned. "Someone has something to gain from this. Something I'm not thinking of..." She trailed off suddenly.

"What? Your eyes—they did that thing."

"What thing?"

"You know who did it!"

Artemis considered this for a moment. And then she tucked her tongue in the side of her cheek, her voice low. "Someone was stealing photo albums from the Watkins'. Someone stole Jeb's phone."

"Who steals photos?"

"*Old* photos."

"Who steals those?"

"Someone interested in old things," Artemis said simply. And then she smiled and slowly lifted her phone. She opened her device, scrolled down, paused, and then her smile turned into a smirk. Just as quickly, though, the realization settling, she went still.

"You know who did it?" Jamie said. Then he answered his question. "You know who did it."

Artemis said, "I know who did it." And then she turned, breaking into a jog, running back into the rain, her phone already placing a call. "Sorry!" she called over her shoulder, spinning as she ran, nearly stumbling backwards, and giving an awkward little wave as she pirouetted in the rain. Then she picked up speed again.

It wasn't until she was five paces from the parking lot that she realized she'd taken a taxi.

"Shit! Jamie—Jamie, I'm so sorry. Could I get a ride?"

Jamie Kramer came to her rescue, hurrying from the gazebo as well, raising his car keys. The lights on an SUV parked neatly between the yellow lines, flashed. Jamie and Artemis both hurried towards the vehicle.

All the while, Artemis willed her phone to connect. "Wade?" she said quickly. "Hey—can you hear me? Yes... I—I think I know who did it. Yes—yes, I need you to look up an address. Right now. Thanks."

CHAPTER 21

Artemis stood behind Forester and Wade, peering over their shoulders at the door to the small bungalow. A red door. A quaint door. Paint along the walls covering chipped sections. A friendly *Welcome* mat on the ground. A pair of shoes set neatly by the front door. No car in the driveway, but the garage was closed.

She tapped her foot nervously on the second, blue-painted wooden step.

Forester and Wade shot quick looks towards where she fidgeted uncomfortably.

"You're sure about this?" Wade murmured. Forester hadn't spoken to her in the brief trip from the curb to the front door.

Jamie Kramer was parked four blocks away, far enough to keep him safe.

"I'm eighty percent sure," Artemis murmured.

Wade shrugged. "Good enough," he muttered. He unholstered his firearm, pounded the door with his fist. "FBI, open up!" Quieter, Wade muttered to Forester. "You check his workplace?"

"Mhmm. Self-employed," Forester said with a quick nod. "Author."

Artemis nodded. This checked out. And it also explained everything. She waited, desperate, certain he wouldn't be home. Certain he'd seen them coming, somehow.

The FBI would think she was a fool. Would think she'd made a terrible mistake. Would think—

Creak. The hinges protested as the door opened.

And a man stood in the doorway, wearing a green sweater vest, glasses and holding a small glass of iced tea. The man looked to be in his sixties, with a faint combover. He was barefoot and smiling congenially.

"Hello," he said, cheerful. "Did you say *FBI*?" He took a sip from his glass, the dark liquid sloshing, ice clinking.

She stared at him. He glanced at each of them quizzically. His eyes never lingered on anyone too long. But of course, she recognized him from his picture on the blog.

The same blog she'd found when searching the internet for mention of the Watkins land. The same blog from an amateur prospector attempting to advertise his self-published panhandling almanac. She remembered reading on the blog how the man had dug on the property for a couple of years before, looking for gold but finding none. A sham, he'd called it. The information presented had citations from news articles dating back to the 1850s.

More importantly, though, she remembered the *other* item he'd advertised.

An upcoming *tell-all* book about the sordid secrets of the Watkins family. "You're John Kordan?"

Another quizzical smile. His glass lowered now. "Mhmm, that's right. Can I help you?"

"Sir," Forester said, "we'd like to speak with you."

He didn't hesitate. Didn't resist. Just nodded, happily. "Want to come in? It's a bit chilly out there, isn't it. Brr." He rubbed at his arms, sloshing some iced-tea. "Oh, whoops. Sorry, guys. Here, come in—just, I'll get that with a towel later. Don't worry. Come on in!" He gestured with one hand, and then turned, leading the way into his house.

Forester and Wade shot Artemis another speculative look. She could see the doubt in their eyes. But she sighed, steeled herself, and stepped into the house of the man she suspected of being the Professor.

The man she believed had killed almost seventy people.

The man, if the witnesses were to be believed, who knew her as *little* Artemis.

Another chill trembled up her arms. The two agents flanked her, and they sidled through the door, over the stain of iced tea on the ground, and through a very neat, well-kept living room with a tidy blue couch, two love seats and a small coffee table displaying a wildlife almanac.

The man was sitting at a dining room table, in an adjoining room, divided by a small, half-wall with a marble top.

He had pulled out three other seats and gestured towards them. "Want some tea? Water?"

No one responded. Forester sat nearest Mr. Kordan. Wade sat on the other side, hand still hovering near his holster. Artemis sat across the table, steepling her hands. Next to the dining room table, she spotted a shelf filled with books. Many of them on various gold rushes throughout history. Others on the Civil War.

"History fan?" he asked her, raising his pale eyebrows.

Again, she didn't reply.

"Not very chatty folks, are you?" he said, giving a good-natured laugh.

This finally eked a response out of Forester. The tall man studied Mr. Kordan, then said, "We'd like to ask you about your whereabouts."

"Sure, when? And just to be upfront, I *am* self-employed. I tend to spend most of my time in the back room at my laptop. Typing away, you know." He laughed again.

"So you can't tell us where you were the last two nights?"

"Here," he said. "Like always. I run a blog."

"I've seen your blog," Artemis interrupted.

"Oh? You're a fan?"

"No," she said, glaring at him. "Why are you playing this game? Stop acting. I know who you are."

Agent Wade shifted uncomfortably. Forester leaned back, looking impressed more than anything. Mr. Kordan gave an uncomfortable little smile, clearing his throat. "I'm... sorry, dear? What do you mean?"

"I'm not your *dear*, you absolute piece of shit." Artemis didn't blink. "I wasn't sure it was you. Eighty percent. Now I'm at ninety. You're too friendly. You know why we're here."

His smile slipped some more. He lifted his glass of tea again, taking a longer sip. "I'm... I'm afraid I don't understand, little missy."

At least that was an improvement. From dear to *little missy*. The man was clearly in his late fifties. Plenty of time to have been active thirty years ago.

"You're the one who stole their photo albums," Artemis said simply. "I looked on your blog again. You have pictures of the

Watkins family going back a hundred years. Pictures with the same coloration and tone that I saw in Isabel's hidden box of photos."

"Come again?"

"You," she said, leaning forward, "asshole, *stole* those pictures. They aren't anywhere else online. You stole them. That's how you have them. You also stole Jeb Arthur's phone two years ago. On your blog, it says two years ago you tried prospecting in the mountains. You were there. You stole his phone. But you were on that land before. Every time you dumped a body."

"Whoa, hang on. Miss, what do you think I did?" He looked stunned. He shot a quick glance towards Forester with a little tilt of his eyebrows. He looked back at Artemis. "Ma'am, I do *not* mean to offend you. But..." he trailed off. "You're confused. I didn't do any of that. Please, now, let's keep inside voices, okay? You can walk me through this stuff. I'll help figure it out. Just, please, we can be polite, right?"

"Shut up," she snapped. She was sick of this. Of men like this. She said, "You used the phone you stole to lure Jeb Arthur to the barn. You knew we'd find him there. You even hid one of your victims in the basement of the ranch."

"I don't know what you're talking about, ma'am. But come on, guys. Let's calm down a second."

Wade was shifting uncomfortably, shooting Artemis hesitant looks. Forester, though, looked as if he was at a movie theater and enjoying himself, his eyes dancing back and forth between Artemis and John Kordan.

"You've been on Watkins land for decades," she said. "Watching, biding your time. The photos, the stolen phone... The *sordid secrets* in your upcoming tell-all... That was going to be the retirement fund, right? You wanted the land, too. Why, exactly? To get the bonafides for the book? Credibility? The man who owns Watkins land revealing secrets of serial killers and tycoons? Is that it?"

"I mean... I'd like the book to do well. But, you know, just gotta keep plugging away, I guess."

"No. Bullshit. You wanted to sell that book. Wanted to bid on that land to drop the prices. What? Hoping to sell it again later? Give tours of the mineshafts and the spots where the bodies are buried? What I want to know is why the Watkins? Why wait this long to go after them? Carl's death, is that it? Isabel changing the will? What's so important about that land, Mr. Kordan. Is there gold on it?"

"No gold," he said quickly. "I don't know about any of the rest of that nonsense—pardon me. I don't mean to be rude. But really, lady, you're off the reservation. But I can *promise* you, there's no gold on that mountain. I've looked. Others have too. The Watkins family, for generations, lured and duped people into thinking there was."

Artemis watched him quietly, studying him closely.

He folded his hands quizzically. "Iced tea?"

"No thank you," Wade said. He shot a look towards Artemis, expectantly.

And this was the difficult part.

Proof.

She needed proof. But she only had conjecture. She knew she was right. Looking at the man, with his neat combover, his sweater-vest. It was all too much. He'd stolen the photos. He'd stolen the phone number. He'd been involved in it all.

He wanted the land. Wanted a tell-all payday. Wanted to pin his own crimes on Jeb Arthur and Eli Watkins.

But he was the killer. She knew he was. She could see it in his posture. In the way he watched them. The easy, over-confident attitude.

"I mean, want me to come downtown with you gentlemen?" he said quickly, glancing at Wade and Forester. "I don't mind. We can discuss more there. Feel free to search my house, my car. Please, just try not to break anything." He gave a little chuckle. "It's not much, but I call it home."

Soulless.

She frowned. The killer had called Isabel Watkins, the grandmother, *soulless*. It had been personal. But why?

For decades... the murders had continued.

Mr. Kordan was now rising slowly from his seat. He gestured over his shoulder. "Mind if I grab a jacket? It's a bit nippy. You can cuff me after, I don't mind."

"Please," Artemis muttered.

Forester was already pulling his handcuffs. Wade still looked uncomfortable.

Suddenly Artemis said, "Wait."

They all looked at her. She raised her phone, displaying the recording. "I've been recording this conversation," she said quietly.

They just frowned at her.

"We have two women who heard your voice, Mr. Kordan. You may be right. I might not have much proof. But I know you did it—and so do they. What are the odds, John, that when I play the recording for them, with police present, that they fail to recognize you, hmm?"

She lowered her phone, staring straight across the table.

He stared back. Wade looked a bit relieved now, nodding. Forester watched Mr. Kordan. The man wasn't smiling so much anymore. He swallowed. His tongue darted out, tasting his lips. Artemis smirked. "Got you. You know I do. Never should have let them go, John. They're going to put you away forever." She narrowed her eyes, feeling the same vicious surge of triumph as she had when telling her father they'd discovered "Easy" the nickname of a guard he'd been bribing. It was only a matter of time for the warden to suss out *who* Otto had been bribing. The why would follow.

And now, she said, "Besides... They're going to go through your computers. Look at those files—manuscripts, research. All of it. They'll find out the truth soon enough. Especially since you just mentioned you work from home. Probably they'll start in your office." She leaned back. "But the voice... I bet you that alone will get a warrant."

John smiled now, nodding slowly. Then, still standing, his tone shifted a bit. "Little Artemis," he said. And suddenly he looked older. His features more gaunt. His eyes *far* heavier, like balls of lead. He said, slowly. "Clever. I always knew you were." He tilted his head. The transformation had reached his posture too. He stood a bit taller now. A bit prouder. A tilt to his head.

"But not as clever as you think," he said simply. "Eleazar Watkins was the original killer. Murdered about twenty of them. He was the one who killed my old man. Lured our family north on the promise of gold. Said he'd sell that mountain to my dad. You want to know why that empty mountain is mine? Because I earned it. My dad earned it. It belongs to us." He spoke slowly, conversationally. Both agents were now rising as well, reaching for their weapons and cuffs. Artemis just sat straight-postured in her chair at the edge of the long table. Mr. Kordan continued, conversationally. She could now hear something of the sing-song quality she'd detected over the phone. And her skin prickled. "Didn't blame him, though. My old man was an ass—he deserved killing. Mr. Watkins thought I'd turn him in. I got away before he could do me. It's all in the book, you know. It will make me millions. The first full-length non-fiction by a serial killer at large."

"Sir," Wade said slowly. "Hands, please."

Kordan ignored him, continuing, "But I never told a soul about Watkins killing my dad. Mr. Watkins took me under his wing... Showed me the ropes. Quite literally." A chuckle. "I had a few playthings of my own. Some of them I killed. Others, I didn't. Then," he smirked. "the student became the master. I killed Mr. Watkins. He ruined my life, after all. Tricking my old man, luring us away from my home on empty promises. Empty mineshafts. An empty mountain. No gold, there, Artemis Blythe. None."

And that was when Artemis spotted it.

Forester, pushing his chair away, reaching towards the professed killer. Wade with cuffs in hand.

But the glass in Mr. Kordan's hand.

It wasn't emptier than when they'd arrived. He'd been taking sips, hadn't he?

But no... He'd been tilting the glass. The liquid had never touched his lips. And then, suddenly, Mr. Kordan moved. He flung the contents of his glass into Forester's eyes. The rest of it found Wade's eyes.

A sudden hiss. Both men screamed, their hands shooting instinctively to their faces. Kordan wasn't done, though. As Artemis scrambled to her feet, the agents yelling, Kordan shoved the long table. She'd sat directly opposite him. Which meant, as he shoved, the wood caught her in the stomach, sending her toppling over the back of her chair.

She heard a smashing sound as she toppled, glimpses where the empty glass was slammed into Forester's skull.

This sent Forester, eyes still steaming, reeling and gasping in pain, stumbling onto the table. Kordan then reached into Forester's holster, yanked out the gun, raised it and shot Wade twice in the chest.

He then turned it, pointing it at Forester's head.

"No!" Artemis screamed, struggling to her feet.

Kordan smirked and pulled the trigger.

But too slow.

Forester had felt the gun against his head. He jerked sideways, and the bullet missed, burying into the table. At the same time, completely blinded, Agent Forester kicked out with a back leg. He caught the old man in the gut, bending him double.

Kordan yelled, trying to aim again. But Artemis had recovered and she flung the closest thing at hand. One of the books from the shelf. She hit Kordan in the face. He missed his second shot at Forester. Now, with a snarl, he aimed, firing at her.

Twice more.

One hit another book—a giant, thick tome on the California gold rush. The bullet didn't make it through. The other missed completely as Forester lunged back, slamming his head into the man's nose.

Blood erupted. The gun fell, skittering under the table. Wade was motionless where he'd toppled, the seat falling to the ground.

Kordan, bloody-nosed, struggled back now.

Acid. That's what had been in the glass. Acid—that's what the survivor had seen in the killer's lair.

The horror of the moment failed to settle as Artemis, breathing heavily, stared at the killer.

The man had distanced from Forester—who, though blinded, at least temporarily—was kicking and bucking, trying to catch the killer. Kordan snorted, spewing droplets of blood. He held a hand to his nose, fury in his eyes.

He stood away from the dining table, away from Forester's writhing form. And Forester had now been blocked by a chair, his leg having smashed through the back. The thing acted as something of a bear trap while he helplessly tried to lash out, blind and in agony.

Artemis stood still, by the bookcase, breathing heavily as the killer regarded her, breathing heavily, distanced from Forester.

Their eyes met. He winked.

Artemis didn't know what was about to happen. Her dread, terror, filled her. Her lungs felt ready to burst. She could feel a surge of horror at where Wade had toppled, shot twice, blinded. Where Forester continued, ferociously, like a wounded animal, to struggle blindly.

And yet, another dread filled her.

An unknowing sort.

"Did you kill Helen?" Artemis whispered. "Helen Blythe. Did you kill her?"

"Kill her?" the man snorted. "Helen Blythe was *not* empty-minded. She deserved to live. I didn't kill her. No. Now you give me something, Artemis." He smiled again, despite the blood pouring down his nose, the noises of pain filling the room.

"What... what do you want, you bastard!"

"Respect," he said quietly. "After all, in a way, you are the way you are because of me. Eli Watkins showed me the ropes. And I returned the favor, to another prospect." He sighed softly, shaking his head. "Didn't turn out quite as well as I'd hoped, granted. But you? Artemis, you'd do *great.*"

She stared at him, stunned. "You... you knew my dad?"

"What are the kids saying these days? *Duh.*"

"The Professor..." she trailed off. "You taught the Ghost-killer?"

"I'd like to linger and chat. But I've got to get going. Keep an eye out for my book, will you? Also—" A pause, another grin. "Because I like you... you want to find Helen? Ask your brother Tommy about the incident at the waterfall. About a year *after* you left. Anyway, ta-ta."

And then he turned, breaking into a sprint, racing through the back of the house.

Artemis wanted to follow. Wanted to give chase.

But then she shot a quick look towards Forester. She didn't know what type of acid had been used. But she knew if she didn't flush his eyes with water and *fast,* the damage would likely be permanent. Hell, for all she knew, it already was.

But Wade was shot. Forester in pain.

And yet... he hadn't killed Helen. That's what she'd wanted to know. Was he lying?

Was he lying about teaching her father?

She wanted to chase him down. To shake answers out of him.

Another growl of pain from Forester.

She cursed beneath her breath. A back door slammed. Then she broke into a sprint. Not after Kordan but towards the sink.

She poured water, testing it, then placed another glass under. "Coming, Cam, hang on!"

Some things, she'd decided, were more important than pursuing the bad guy.

She rushed back to Forester, tilting his head. "Hang on—open your eyes. I know it hurts!"

"Shit, Checkers," Forester gasped through gritted teeth. "You know what you're doing?"

"Not at all."

"Great."

"Hold on."

Suddenly, another sound. More gasping. A groan.

"Hang on—Wade?" Forester yelled.

A grunt. "Chest," he replied. "Vest." A long groan.

"Shit, thank God," Forester said. "You still owe me for that pizza. Not gonna let you skimp out!"

"Cam?" Wade called.

"Mhmm?"

"Shut the hell up."

Artemis felt a huge surge of relief. Wade was alive. At least there was that. "Forester, this is water. Tip it, all right. Rinse your eyes."

"Got it. This punishment for being wrong about Jeb?"

"No—just do it, Cam. I'm going to help Wade."

She raced back into the kitchen, gasping, her spine tingling. She poured another glass, returned to the living room and dropped next to Wade's side. He'd received less of the concoction than Forester and only one of his eyes was closed. The other blinked rapidly, taking her in and wincing.

"Where's the killer?" he demanded.

"Gone," she said.

Wade cursed, fishing for his phone. Artemis pushed his hand down. "Later—flush your eye. Please!"

"Call backup."

"I will. If you flush your—"

"Fine!" Wade snapped.

"See?" Cam called out across the table. "She's annoying sometimes, isn't she?"

"Shut up," Wade and Artemis both shouted at him.

While the men poured water, Artemis dialed 9-1-1 and raced back into the kitchen to grab another glass. And another.

Back and forth, she raced, carrying water to the FBI agents. And all the while, she could only count as minutes ticked by.

Kordan had gotten away.

And there was nothing she could do to bring him back. He'd known her father. Known her family. He'd... he'd taught her father how to kill? Was it true?

She shuddered.

It was bad enough to have a killer who knew her name behind bars. But to have one out and about, lurking in every shadow? Her stomach tightened. And she sprinted back into the living room, balancing another glass of water.

The killer's words lingered. He'd uttered them with contempt, with amusement. But they echoed like gunshots in her mind. *You want to find Helen? Ask your brother Tommy about the incident at the waterfall. About a year after you left. Anyway, ta-ta.*

Did Tommy know something about Helen?

Why hadn't he told her?

Artemis shook her head, trying to focus on the task at hand, shuttling glasses of water while trying to bark instructions into her phone, directing the police to the bungalow.

You want to find Helen?

If Tommy had been hiding something...

One way or another, she would *make* him talk.

The End

WANT TO KNOW MORE?

Greenfield press is the brainchild of bestselling author Steve Higgs. He specializes in writing fast paced adventurous mystery and urban fantasy with a humorous lilt. Having made his money publishing his own work, Steve went looking for a few 'special' authors whose work he believed in.

Georgia Wagner was the first of those, but to find out more and to be the first to hear about new releases and what is coming next, you can join the Facebook group by typing the link below into your browser .

WHAT IS NEXT FOR ARTEMIS BLYTHE?

SHE'S ALL ALONE

Genius Chessmaster and FBI consultant Artemis Blythe is now suspected of murder, accused of picking off competition in her upcoming tournament. The evidence is iron clad. They have her on camera entering the room of the most recent murder victim *minutes* before he died.

The FBI is sent to arrest her, and Artemis is forced to flee, running to her brother—who has ties to the Seattle mob—in order to lay low. It's now a race against time for Artemis to clear her name and find the real killer before the FBI locates her.

But time spent with her twin brother yields clues to another case—the disappearance of their sister, seventeen years ago. In a shocking climax, Artemis learns once and for all: what happened to Helen? All the while tackling her most mind-bending case yet.

GEORGIA WAGNER

AN ARTEMIS BLYTHE MYSTERY THRILLER

BOOK 5

SHE'S ALL ALONE

Printed in Great Britain
by Amazon

42477013R00126